<u>*Advance Praise for Gorman's House*</u>

"This coming-of-age story is a nostalgic Halloween treat for '90s kids who grew up on haunted houses, horror movies, and urban legends!"

—Ally Russell, author of *It Came From the Trees*

"Fast paced, creepy and packed with references, Gorman's House is a spooky 90s delight you won't want to miss. T. T. Madden delivers a haunting story of teens looking for themselves lured into an old Gothic manor inside a dead mall where they would have to face fears way more terrifying than the creature trying to devour them."

—J. V. Gachs, author of *Epiphany* and *Unholy*

"It really doesn't get much better than a story that takes place on a '90s Halloween night in a mysterious haunted house—like, front door, shutters, and all—that pops up in an abandoned mall. Except it does, because Madden's writing makes you feel right at home with every nostalgic, deep cut reference, right before pulling the rug out from under you with warped horror that sticks with you for days."

—Kristen Rogers-Anderson, co-host of *Guide to the Unknown*

"Inventive and endlessly charming with the ways that it evokes 90s nostalgia, all while being seat-of-your-pants scary. You've never seen a haunted house like this."

—Chloe Spencer, author of *CodeSkull*

"*Gorman's House* is a terrifying trip of 90s nostalgia through an evil, sentient location. It's Goosbumps meets Shirtly Jackson."

—Rachel Bolton, Bram-Stoker-Award©-nominee

For a moment, after looking upon the house, Danny wanted to leave more than anything in the world. There wasn't just an eerie feeling about it, not just something minorly unsettling, but a terror, deep and real, that told him to run, run for the hills.

In less than an hour, he'd be telling himself he should've listened to that voice, he should've run.

They all should've run.

Gorman's House

MADAXEMEDIA.COM

Published by Mad Axe Media

madaxemedia.com

The Totally Freaked! series is an original creation of Mad Axe Media.

Edited by Joey Powell

Book Cover & Interior Design by Joey Powell

Print ISBN: 978-1-966497-02-8

E-Book ISBN: 978-1-966497-03-5

For all the Black kids who were never on the front of
books when we were little.

Chapter One
"Mischief Night"

October 30th, 199X; The town of Beacon refuses to come into the 21st century, squarely planted in the temporal ambiguity of 199X. There are no fiber optic cables, no cell phones nestled in pockets, no internet fads, or even combination VHS/DVD players. It is an age of neighborhood bicycles, old playing cards *fap-ap-ap*-ing in their spokes. Of bubble-fronted televisions that make a loud click and soft hum as they turn on. It's the age of landlines, of calling around, of a dismissal bell announcing complete and total freedom.

It is Mischief Night.

Beacon was a town that had its fair share of action after nightfall, especially around Halloween, when mischief infected the air itself. This action was always of the relatively innocent kind; teenagers out past curfew, lying in fields and dreaming of the future, popping in VHS tapes at sleepovers and settling in for a night of scary movies, or making out in the backseats of cars if they were older.

But this was something different.

The thing that stirred at the edge of town was neither local nor ordinary.

Nor was it innocent.

It was something ancient and foreign, not just to the town of Beacon, but to this very realm of existence. Something even darker than the midnight dark, that waited in the woods around town. And while that dark presence waited, it sent a version of itself, an emissary, out into the world.

The Stranger carried all the menace of the dark presence with him, a feeling that was quite distinct from all the mischief and Halloween in the air. As he walked through town, a shadow darker than the dark, the teenagers out lying in fields were suddenly overcome with an existential dread over their futures. The children watching scary movies found something much more violent and dreadful was burned into their

VHS tapes, something that looked shockingly real. The makeout sessions shriveled up and ended. Those at home found themselves unable to sleep, thinking dark, intrusive thoughts as they stared at the ceilings above their beds. The Stranger knew he had this effect on the town, on anyplace he went, and he delighted in it. Beneath his wide-brimmed hat, he smiled a crooked, toothy smile.

The Stranger walked a nonsensical route throughout Beacon, coming out of the woods around the abandoned Northfield Mall and wandering winding, circuitous paths down streets, alleyways, across lawns, through parking lots and backyard bushes, leaving a trail everywhere he went. But this trail was not muddy footprints or scuff marks, not broken branches or burst jack-o'-lanterns.

No, the Stranger dropped trinkets everywhere he went. Seemingly at random, seemingly going unnoticed by him. A scroll fell from beneath his long, dark coat, a rolled-up paper sealed with wax. He dropped what appeared to be a label-less burned CD. A Rubik's cube, but in a strange black-and-gold coloration, and without any squares, just arcane designs. A golden astrolabe, intertwined, spinning discs at its center. A folded-up truck-stop map. A cartridge for a video game console. A book in an unknown language. A flyer with tear-away phone numbers at the bottom. A VHS tape. Hundreds of bits of detritus fell from the folds of his coat, an impossible amount of things for him to actually have on him, and he just left them strewn all around Beacon.

Just as mysteriously as the Stranger appeared, he vanished, disappearing into an alley behind the strip mall that held the town's booming Blockbuster, swallowed by the dark.

The van full of monsters drove around the town of Beacon, knowing exactly the kind of mischief they were about to get into. Because underneath those monstrous masks were the star players of Beacon High School's football team. In the back of the van there was the Gimp from *The People Under the Stairs*, Chucky himself (of course, the stitched-up version from the new *Bride of Chucky*), and the titular Leprechaun. Between them were dozens of cartons of eggs and packages of toilet paper they were in the process of opening. Cans of spray paint clattered around the van at their feet.

"We're almost there," said the driver, Hannibal Lecter, who was really Jason Marshal, the team captain and quarterback. The Hannibal mask was the one that obscured the eyes the least, and so naturally had to go to the driver. Plus, Jason was one of the few of them who actually had his license, and if they got caught, none of them was willing to risk whatever punishment would come from driving without a license on top of whatever egging and TP-ing houses and tagging parks would get them. Jason wore a dark beanie on his head, which wasn't part of the costume, but it covered up the bright flame of red hair that would've easily disclosed his identity.

"You ready?" Jason looked into the rear-view mirror at the monsters in the back, the Gimp, Chucky, and Leprechaun, and then at the final monster in the passenger's seat; the looming facade of the one and only Ghostface. They had all fought over that one. *Scream* was the freshest movie out there, the one that had shaken the horror movie scene up and spawned a dozen ripoffs; *The Faculty, I Know What You Did Last Summer, Urban Legend*, each one of which the majority of Beacon High students had saved up allowance or part-time job money (or in cases like Jason's, just dipped into their inheritance money) to go and see.

Danny Green, the running back under the Ghostface mask, liked all those *Scream* clones just fine, but he was more of a *Tales From the Hood* or *Candyman* kinda guy. *Anaconda* was his jam, he'd practically worn out the VHS. He'd even throw a bone to *Deep Blue Sea*, since Cool lived all the way through that one. Because Danny was one of the few black kids at Beacon High. That meant he was treated as an oddity at the worst of times, and an exotic idol at the best. Both, in his opinion, were equally bad. They just had their different ways of being bad. He wondered if some tangled rats-nest of conflicting emotions in the rest of the team was why everyone conceded to letting him be Ghostface so easily.

That, plus what had happened with Coach.

Danny told himself he didn't care that much about the why. He got what he wanted, and he wanted to be Ghostface. But another part of him chastised himself for not feeling bad. He tried to put all those complicated thoughts out of his head and focus on the moment, on the night. After all, there was no way he was going to figure out all of this right now, sitting in the passenger's seat of Jason Marshal's older brother's dirty old band van.

They had mischief to get into.

This night in Beacon, October 30th, was called Mischief Night, but the teenage monsters had heard of other names for it as well; Devil's Night, Gate Night. It was something different everywhere, like calling that carbonated beverage *soda* or *pop*. Personally, Danny didn't quite care what the night was called, so long as it meant giving them an opportunity to get one over on Coach.

Coach Walter was less the football team's coach and more of a drill sergeant. He looked like he might've stepped right out from the Army and into their school, a buff, older white dude who'd rather shave his head than be seen to be going bald. He was built like the kind of guy who played criminals in 40s crime movies, a brick wall of a man. Just like with every other teacher in Beacon High, Coach had his eye on Danny far more than the other kids. As if he expected him to mess up. Like he knew trouble would be coming from Danny and nobody else. He watched Danny on the field, in the hall, his gaze ever-present, as if daring him.

And then earlier that week, at practice, Coach had finally put hands on him. It wasn't a hit, a strike, but

Coach had grabbed Danny roughly by the collar of his uniform, hauled him over to face him. In that moment, Danny had completely forgotten what he'd done to warrant such behavior, forgotten what Coach had even said to him. All he remembered was the man's face turning beet red and the shame of having the rest of the team stare at him afterward. The place where Coach grabbed him felt like it was on fire. It still tingled a little.

Come on, man, Danny told himself, *focus*. He almost hadn't realized the van was slowing down, that they were at the spot. Jason parked the van a block down from Coach's house. All the lights were off. Made sense. It was 11:45. Almost finished with Mischief Night and very nearly Halloween proper. Danny and the other monsters hopped out.

"You better not ditch us," Danny said lowly over his shoulder, though more out of that thing inside himself he tried to push down than any past behavior that would indicate Jason would actually ditch them. Jason was buddy-buddy with the rest of the team, but with Danny it was different. He knew Jason saw him like so many other people did; something new and different. Like an exotic bird in a cage at the zoo. Despite the fact that Danny had lived in Beacon his entire life.

"Come on" Jason smirked through his Hannibal Lecter mask. "He catches half the team and the *quarterback* ain't there?" He had a good point, but the way he said it let Danny know Jason was aware of how everyone else saw him; on a pedestal above all the rest. The rich kid. Quarterback with the head cheerleader girlfriend. The star. The cliche.

"Besides," Jason said, "we've got more stops tonight."

He was right about that too. They still wanted to egg Principal Hill's car, at least.

Danny led the team of monsters forward, staying off the sidewalks and out of the street lights, creeping through backyards in the night, crunching through dried leaves, passing decorative witches and skeletons, stepping around pumpkins both carved and not, plastic tombstones erupting from the earth and sheet-ghosts hanging from trees. When they finally reached Coach Walter's house, they let the place have it, but to Danny it felt ... hollow. There was the natural surge of adrenaline as he pelted an egg or roll of toilet paper (Why wasn't the quarterback—you know, the one with the arm—doing this?), but this small bit of revenge felt empty in a way he couldn't really figure out.

Someone misjudged a throw and hit an upstairs window with a roll of toilet paper. It made a hollow, echoing *thump*, but Danny wasn't about to take any chances.

"Let's get out of here!" he whisper-yelled through the Ghostface mask. It was the right decision, because half a second later a light came on in that window. It was in that moment the real adrenaline finally hit Danny, the feeling he felt he ought to be feeling, and he ran with the other monsters through Coach's yard, out to the sidewalk, a grin on his face.

Down the street, Jason's brother's van lurched forward, speeding up to them and barely slowing down as it rolled up to the sidewalk.

The sound of a heavy front door swinging open.

"Hey, you!" Coach shouted from behind them as the monsters all threw themselves into the van. "Get back here, you little shits!"

"Gun it!" Danny shouted.

Jason slammed on the gas just as Danny cranked the stereo up. The wheels burned rubber onto the street as the Beastie Boys hollered "Sabotage" from the van's cassette so loudly they rattled the windows and blew the speakers out.

Across town, Kennedy Parsons closed her eyes and listened to the sound of the skateboard trucks, the wheels spinning against the concrete, the wooden boards grinding against rails. She didn't think there was any more beautiful sound in the world, except maybe the music that had come along with them. Someone had brought a boombox to the skate park, along with a few mixtapes, and the Cranberries were the current soundtrack to all the skate moves.

God, this was so much better than stupid cheer practice.

Kennedy opened her eyes and looked down at herself, at the clothes that were so unlike her and yet felt so right. The big, dark boots and ripped jeans. The bandanna tied around her left knee, the red flannel shirt that was far too big for her over a faded Veruca Salt T-shirt. Her blond hair was back in a ponytail, and instead of the bright, sassy makeup she normally wore, her eyes were dark-rimmed and grunge, nails black instead of pastel.

If anyone from the cheer squad saw her in this outfit they would seriously freak.

And yet she'd never felt more at home.

This was the Kennedy she wanted to be.

Skaters spun through the park around her, some in costume even for Mischief Night, some not, some halfway, masks perched on the crowns of their heads. She saw Michael Myers and Ace Ventura in a tutu and a couple Rugrats, and even an MC Hammer, and marveled at how difficult it must be to skate in those pants.

Officially, Kennedy was supposed to be going for Halloween as Evelyn from *The Mummy*, and while she'd already put together the costume, already tried it on and found herself quite pretty in it, there was something about it that sent spikes of anxiety through her, made her feel the same way she felt when she had to put on her cheer uniform. Her going as Evelyn made sense, because Jason Marshal, the football captain, was going as Rick. Though they weren't a couple (yet), everyone was sure Jason was going to ask Kennedy out on Halloween.

The thought made her stomach flip.

And not in a good way.

She heard the growl of trucks and wheels and a sudden rush of wind and then a "Glad you decided to come out tonight" at her side and she looked up into the face of Ryan King and all that nervous anxiety for the future was blown away.

To be replaced with the much more immediate anxiety of being in Ryan's presence.

Ryan was the queen of the alt kids around Beacon. Her short hair was done in a pixie cut, and she had a couple small, silver hoops in each ear. She wore a flannel tied around her waist, Vans, and ripped jeans. She was practically swimming in a Foo Fighters T-shirt that hid her small boobs. At any passing glance, and with that name, Ryan might be able to pass for a boy. But there was something inside Kennedy that was keenly aware Ryan was very much not a boy, something inside her that was keenly aware she felt for Ryan what she was supposed to feel for boys (for Jason). Kennedy was hyper-aware of the fullness of Ryan's lips, of how bright her pretty, green eyes shone, of the way the tied flannel emphasized her hips. She felt herself get hot and pushed that strange feeling down.

"Huh?" Kennedy asked, wondering why she got so tongue-tied whenever Ryan was nearby. *But you know why, don't you?*

"I said glad you could come out tonight," Ryan said, sitting down next to Kennedy. "You're probably gonna be all booked up tomorrow."

"Yeah ..." Kennedy thought of herself in her Evelyn costume, standing next to the dashing Jason. The thought *looked* nice, but it didn't *feel* like anything. Sitting there with Ryan on the other hand, felt ...

Like what?

It feels like how they say it's supposed to feel.

But what was that *it*? She knows, but she can't bring herself to say.

"You okay?" Ryan touched her on the shoulder, and Kennedy's heart jumped into her throat.

"Yeah, I'm okay," she said, though she was very much not.

The distant growl of an engine distracted her and then bore itself into her brain as it grew louder, closer. The skaters around them stopped or slowed as equally-loud music announced the arrival of a dark van speeding through on a cross-street. The Beastie Boys hollered as loud as the boys inside the van, tires screeching as they turned past the skate park and headed toward the outskirts of town. Kennedy recognized the van as Jason's older brother's. It was always parked in the driveway whenever she went over to his house.

"There's always someone," Ryan said.

"Yeah," Kennedy said distantly. But the van had already left her mind, replaced by her memory of the end of *The Mummy*, of Evelyn in chains.

Chapter Two
Halloween

When Danny dressed for school on Halloween morning, it was in fancier clothes than he had worn in a long time. Sure, he always dressed up at least a little for picture day and always had to put on something nice before football games, but dressing in fancy clothes was something new for Halloween. This year he didn't go to a costume store, didn't save up his money to get something big and elaborate he'd only wear for one night and then never again. Instead, he'd raided his dad's closet and found everything he'd needed in sizes that he was growing into quicker than he'd expected. A small part of him wondered if that meant he was really becoming an adult, but he pushed that part down, determined to enjoy what he knew would be a day of little actual responsibilities.

Danny came out of his father's closet with a faded yellow shirt, brown suspenders, brown dress shoes, and light-colored slacks. He obviously didn't have access to a gunbelt, so he'd tied a couple of brown belts together and looped them around his shoulders to emulate a shoulder rig. He thought it came out alright. He didn't wanna mess with his fade, so, hair aside, he found himself looking into the mirror at a pretty decent image of Danny Glover's character, Mike Harrigan, from *Predator 2*.

Danny had seen the first *Predator* at a sleepover a few years ago. There were a couple guys at the Blockbuster who didn't check ID and would let you just take out whatever. Jason had checked that one out and had most of the first stringers over to his place after a particularly tough span of losses. He thought it would bring them all together, and he was right. The first one had Carl Weathers and Bill Duke, sure, and all the other kids on the team had loved Arnold, but that movie hadn't really done it for Danny in the way some other movies had. He'd enjoyed the experience with his teammates, all hidden down in Jason's basement, the big bubble television casting a blue glow out onto them, the volume down low so as not to wake Jason's parents. But the movie itself was not much for him to sink his teeth into. Great monster, but a buncha white guys in the jungle, all the brown people dying first, dying horribly, as they often did in horror movies.

Predator 2, now that was where it was at. Danny Glover at the center of the action, a big city instead of a jungle, cops and gangsters instead of soldiers and some international intrigue plot he didn't really care about happening half a world away. The second one was much more connected to Danny's own reality (not to mention the fact that there was the appearance of the Alien skull, which sent all his friends into theory-crafting mode).

Danny threw his backpack on and began his walk to school, satisfied with his costume.

He wasn't sure if the air truly felt different when he walked outside, or if it was just because it was Halloween. That greatest of holidays always brought a different feeling to the world. And especially this year, with it being on a Friday. Sure, that meant Saturday was November–officially–but what it really meant was Halloween would last an entire weekend. A night and two days full of parties, of friends, of being able to be someone else and not have anyone think twice about it. Danny slowed as that thought crossed his mind. Being someone else. Why had that been so important to him? Why was that one of the first things he thought of?

He would have spent longer on that thought, would have followed it down its road to see where it led, but as he walked, something on the sidewalk glinted right into his eye, harsher and brighter than Danny thought the October sun was capable of. The thing was directly in his path, and as he walked up to it, he saw it was a horizontal cartridge case, like a Nintendo 64 game. The case had duct tape wrapped around the entirety of it, so it was impossible to see what game it was actually for, but Danny recognized the shape; he had dozens of similar boxes on his own shelf.

Danny wedged the case open and slid the contents out into his palm. Sure enough, it was a Nintendo 64 cartridge. But whatever game it was for was impossible to tell; the label had been peeled off, only that sticky, white underside remaining. In its place someone had doodled, in Sharpie, a small drawing of what looked like a house. Creepy and Gothic, like Dracula's castle, with spires and looming eye-like windows.

Danny felt a strange draw to the cartridge. For all he knew it was trash, and yet not only had he found himself compelled to pick it up, but to keep it. Danny lifted his head and looked around, and yet saw no one around who could have dropped the case. No one who it might belong to. He slid the case into his backpack, and found himself thinking about it the entire walk to school.

The bait had been spread throughout the hunting ground. The traps had been set. The dark presence lurked in the shape of a house. Its front door opened on slow, creaky hinges as it got ready to welcome the first of its visitors into its maw.

Kennedy looked at her homemade Evie Carnahan costume hanging on the closet door.

"Nah," she said aloud, definitively, riding the wave of feeling that had been sitting with her since last night, since she spent Mischief Night with the alt kids—with Ryan—listening to the Foo Fighters and skating instead of with the cheer squad, listening to the Spice Girls and drinking pilfered wine coolers. That feeling of being trapped, of the Evie costume closing in around her, the thought of being somewhere at a party only for Jason to find her, to corner her in that way that boys so often do. Put their arm up against a wall in front of you. To physically trap you in a place without even realizing they're doing it, like it's a move they've all been taught.

Kennedy went into her big sister's room and right to her dresser. Carrie was off at college, and wouldn't miss the couple of small items Kennedy needed to complete her last-minute costume. She already had the T-shirt and brown shorts she needed, but from Carrie's room she took a pair of big, brown boots, some stockings, as many bracelets and necklaces as she could find, and a couple tube socks. She rifled through the downstairs closet for her dad's fishing vest, and when she was finished putting them all together, she had a pretty impressive Tank Girl.

Everyone at school thought so too.

The way people looked at her, Kennedy could tell they didn't even realize who she was. Not the costume, everyone knew who Tank Girl was—but underneath. She heard a few people gasp her name and only saw the looks of realization on their faces when she spoke or waved to them, intentionally revealing her existence as Kennedy Parsons. She was so busy fantasizing about what Ryan would have to say when she finally found her that she wasn't even thinking of Jason. She basked instead in the Halloween of it all, everyone else in their own costumes, the cut-out witches and bats and plastic pumpkins and leaves and cornucopias all over the school.

The looks of all her fellow students made her think of the end of *The Faculty*, one of the few parts she found herself really not caring for but in a way she was never able to properly articulate. She didn't mind that Stokely started to date Stan, but she did mind she upended her entire personality to do it. Everyone seemed so fine with that. Everyone seemed to *prefer* it. But it made Kennedy irrationally angry. She knew such a transformation was a trope in lots of 80s movies her mom watched, and she didn't care for it there either.

She passed the cheer squad on her way to homeroom, and when she waved at them, she realized she didn't know who a single one of them was dressed as, and the vast gulf between her and them became so much clearer.

"Mr. Green!"

The call had come from Dr. Gunn, Beacon High's only black teacher (not counting the occasional substitute). Dr. Gunn was one of the few teachers who always called kids by their last names, and always included the honorific. With Coach, it was always just a top-of-the-lungs *Green!*—when he shouted at Danny, when he grabbed him by the collar—but Dr. Gunn talked to each of his students like they were on the same level.

Dr. Gunn mostly taught the upper-level English courses, the ones that awarded college credits, and he dressed like that was where he belonged. He always wore a tweed suit that made him look like a man out of time, a professor from the 1800s or something. A few of the younger teachers sometimes tried to dress or act hip to get the kids to identify with them, wearing Nirvana T-shirts or talking about how cool whatever the big new movie that month was. But it always came off as exactly what it was. Despite Dr. Gunn's own youth, he seemed to have no interest in that whatsoever, not lowering himself down to talk to the students, but raising the students up to his level.

"Mr. Green, I'd like to see you for a moment."

"Yes, sir," Danny said, hurrying over. Before he even got there, Dr. Gunn held open the door to his classroom, and Danny knew this was something more serious than a simple chat. He stiffened, straightened, held himself up higher as he crossed the threshold into the classroom. Dr. Gunn set the door ajar behind them, but didn't close it, the noise in the hall blocking out any chance of eavesdropping.

Dr. Gunn's classroom was noticeably different from other rooms in Beacon High. The other classrooms were all decorated with pictures of presidents, long-dead writers and scientists, men who all had one thing in common; their whiteness. Danny had never seen a black man on any wall in Beacon High that wasn't Dr. King or Malcolm, and even then that was usually only ever in February, temporary displays going up to remind students, yes, the Civil Rights Movement existed, had happened. Dr. Gunn's walls on the other hand, had people Danny could see himself in. Dr. King and Malcolm, sure, but also Maya Angelou, Du Bois, Josephine Baker, George Washington Carver, Jackie Robinson. He still hadn't put up that NWA poster Danny had suggested. He didn't think that was gonna happen.

Dr. Gunn studied Danny's costume as he walked into his classroom.

"I'm not sure I know who you are."

As much as Danny wanted to quote a line, he didn't think Dr. Gunn was the best audience. Besides, all the best ones had swears.

"I'm Harrigan from *Predator 2*." And then, when he saw the look on Dr. Gunn's face, he added, "Danny Glover," like the name of a big, respected actor would make it count for more. And he did see a little change on Dr. Gunn's face. It wasn't much, but it might've been enough to get him to at least look at the box the next time he wandered through a Blockbuster.

"Everything okay, Dr. Gunn?" Danny asked.

"Why don't you tell me?" he said, and walked over to his desk. He picked up a piece of paper and held it out before Danny. "I'd like you to explain this to me, Mr. Green."

The paper had Danny's name on it. It was his test, the test they'd taken last week on *The Three Musketeers*. The letter C was written atop it in pencil. Danny's first thought was that Dr. Gunn usually graded in blue pen.

"My ... test?" Danny asked calmly, even though the bottom just dropped out of his stomach. Did he know? No, how could he know? No, of course he knew. He was Dr. Gunn. The man knew everything.

He knew Danny had blown the test on purpose. *Green!*

"From our discussion the other day, it seemed you'd quite enjoyed the novel," Dr. Gunn said, sitting on the edge of his desk.

He wasn't lying. Danny did like it, even though it was one of those old and stuffy books school always made them read. He had to check out one of those versions that was rewritten for younger readers from the library to understand some parts with all the old-timey language, but he enjoyed it. About the only thing he'd liked that school had shown him so far was the *Othello* with Lawrence Fishburne. Although even he had to admit the Leonardo DiCaprio *Romeo + Juliet* wasn't too bad. But despite what the administration might think, men like Ernest Hemingway and Arthur Miller had very little to teach a kid like Danny. They might as well have lived on different planets.

"It was aight," Danny said. And then when he saw the look on Dr. Gunn's face, he corrected himself and said, "*Alright.*"

"There were just enough right answers here," Dr. Gunn said, "to pass the test."

Danny almost said, *Cs get degrees*, something he'd heard from Jason's older brother during one of their many trips through the basement. But those Cs had only been enough to get him into Beacon Community College. Danny, on the other hand, was looking at potential football scholarships. He was possibly looking at free rides. But there was something about that possibility that didn't sit right with him. Something that made him feel weird in a way he couldn't define, like the way the rest of the team looked at him when they conceded the Ghostface mask.

"You have a free period Monday, yes?" Dr. Gunn asked, but it was less of a question.

"Yes, sir."

"Then I'd like you to spend it here, retaking this test."

Danny almost gasped, almost cried out in protest,

but he saw the look in Dr. Gunn's eyes. It wasn't a punishment he was handing down to Danny. Not a stern, towering look, like when Coach made them do sprints as punishment for goofing off. Dr. Gunn's look, this offer, they were lifelines. Danny closed his mouth and stood straighter, looked Dr. Gunn in his eyes.

"Yes, sir," he said. "Monday."

"I'm glad to hear it," Dr. Gunn said, holding out his hand. Danny shook it, and he felt the agreement there, binding them, pulling them together. It was about more than just a test.

"You're smarter than a C, Mr. Green. Don't pretend you're not."

But the implication was clear; *men like us can't afford to.*

Chapter Three
The Game

Danny shouldered open the door to his house and barely remembered to close it, he was so distracted. He did it with his foot, not breaking stride at all. He tossed his backpack down at his seat at the kitchen table, as was his routine, but he already had the cartridge case out, turning it over in his hands, trying to figure it out. It gave up nothing, of course. He'd spent all day looking at it under his desk, taking the cartridge out of the case, turning it over in his hands. Every time he found nothing, but each time he looked at it again he was convinced he'd discover some new secret. The school day passed achingly slowly. Because it was Halloween, yes, as it did every year, that greatest of childhood holidays fell on a school day, but Danny was finally home now, and he hustled through the kitchen to the basement door, grateful his parents weren't home so he wouldn't have to answer any questions about his day, who he was dressed as, his night plans.

Danny's basement was a holy place, a temple to all things nerdy. His parents let him have it mostly to himself, if only, he suspected, because it meant he kept the sounds of *Dragon Ball Z* reruns and video games and the constant whir of the VCR to himself. It was huge, separated from the rest of the house by a turn in the stairs. Down there with him was only the laundry room and a sliding glass door to the backyard. An old couch and a coffee table littered with comics and video game guidebooks set up before a big, CRT television. A desk on the left that was used more for storage, though if Danny moved some things around he could sit down at the computer there. There were stacks of VHS tapes piled haphazardly around the room, from *Leprechaun* to *The Faculty* and *From Dusk Till Dawn*. On either side of the television were towers of video games in the rectangular cardboard cases of Nintendo 64, and the jewel case packaging of PlayStation CDs; all the *Resident Evil* games, *Parasite Eve*, and even a few he really wasn't supposed to have, like *Night Trap* and *Phantasmagoria* (thanks again to the couple guys at the Blockbuster who sold anybody anything).

Danny sat down on the couch and pulled the unlabeled cartridge out of its case. Nothing about it had changed. But it was without a doubt a cartridge that would fit in the N64. He turned on the TV, flipped from a rerun of that new special, *Courage the Cowardly Dog*, to channel 03, making sure the RCA of the Nintendo–the red, yellow, and white cables–was plugged in. He pulled out the last game he was playing, *Doom 64*, and popped the new game in, booting up the console.

He saw the familiar N64 startup screen, and then he finally made it to the game itself. The screen was black, and fading in out of that blackness was a big, pixelated yellow smile that took up most of the screen. The smile widened, and Danny saw more of those ugly, yellow teeth before a haunted house faded into view, accompanied by a spooky 64-bit musical score. The house was classic; an old, gothic look, with boarded-up windows and haunted yellow lights glowing from inside. There was a low laugh of some monstrous thing and the words *Gorman's House* suddenly splattered across the screen, along with the words PRESS START below.

Gorman's House. The name shook something loose in Danny, something he hadn't thought about in a while, so it took him a moment to recover it. Gorman's House was the stuff of urban legends, like Beacon's own supposedly-haunted house, Foxhill Manor, that kids often visited on dares. The kind of thing someone tells you a friend of their cousin who goes to school in a different state said. Danny heard Gorman's House was the name of a haunted attraction that moved from town to town, one that was so scary no one was ever able to complete it. They said the top floor had either huge stacks of cash or some wicked prize as a reward for finishing. They made a movie about it, he remembered, *Chimera House*. He'd rented it from the Blockbuster a while ago. Liked the movie a lot, but never thought the place was real. It was like the rumor people started about the guy in the ice cream truck in their neighborhood who secretly sold drugs on the side.

Did this mean it was true that Gorman's House was real?

Danny already had the controller in his hands, had pressed START, before he'd even finished the thought.

When Danny loaded into the game world, he found himself standing in the front yard of a large mansion. There was no pre-game cutscene, nothing telling him exposition or objectives. He was simply dropped in. He couldn't tell who his character was, exactly, but he figured he was a woman, judging by the ponytail. The avatar was rendered in blocky polygons like Leon and Claire in *Resident Evil 2*, the backgrounds similarly pre-rendered.

Danny tested out the controls and found his character moved similarly to those games. Tank controls. A quick check of the pause menu confirmed his inventory; his avatar had a lockpick, a flashlight, and a readable notebook. Standard survival horror items. The only note in the notebook was *Solve the riddle, find the house.* And then, below that, *Gorman's House, 7780 Paper Street.*

Danny moved his character around the front yard and then into the manor, testing the boundaries of the game. There were locked doors leading to the side yard and different parts of the manor that the game told him required certain keys. A statue with outstretched arms in the foyer that the game said *looks like this ought to be holding something*. A locked foot locker. A bathroom that functioned as a save point.

And, of course, monsters.

Danny couldn't tell what exactly the enemy monsters were supposed to be. They didn't really have a shape to them, just unfinished pixels like MissingNo. in the Pokemon games, moving without any kind of animation. Whenever they grabbed his player character, the entire screen pixelated, he saw that horrid yellow mouth on the GAME OVER screen, and then he found himself back in the last save room. There was no way to fight the monsters, at least not yet, so Danny reloaded and tried again, making his way through the house.

He'd just found a mysterious letter on top of an old desk and was about to read it when there was a hand on his actual real-life shoulder.

"Jesus!" Danny shot up off the couch, tossing his controller halfway across the room. He came around in a squared-up stance, ready to fight, but it was only Jason and Kennedy, standing there behind the couch.

"The hell, man?" Jason said. "We've been calling you. You didn't hear us?"

"No, I ... What are y'all supposed to be?" Danny asked, but he knew. Jason was dressed as Rick O'Connell from *The Mummy*, and ... he didn't know who Kennedy was. But he was damn sure she wasn't Evie.

"What are you playing?" Jason asked, using the opening to blatantly avoid the question. Danny could see on his face their Halloween costume mixup was a sore spot, but he didn't press it. Especially not after he saw the look on Kennedy's face. It didn't look like she'd been crying or anything, but she was very clearly uncomfortable. Something must've happened between them in the car.

"What is this?" Jason asked. He was already down on the couch, the three-pronged N64 controller in his hand, looking at the screen.

"I found it," Danny said, sitting down next to him and smoothing the awkwardness more for Kennedy's sake than Jason's. Whatever was going on between them, he didn't really wanna know. "I found it outside."

"You found it outside," Jason said, clearly in disbelief. He paused the game, looked back at Danny, and raised his eyebrows.

"You know what it is?" Danny asked, trying to hide the smile on his face.

Jason shook his head.

Danny took the controller back from him. He had to pull a little harder than he should've, but Jason relinquished it. Danny quit out to the main menu, not afraid of losing his progress since he'd just found himself in a save room, and let Jason linger on the title screen.

"No," he said, walking the thin line between disbelief and outright denial. He looked away from Danny and to the screen. "No way, what is this?"

"It's exactly what it says, my man," Danny said, gesturing to the screen.

"They never made a game of Gorman's House. A movie, sure. Was just okay, if you ask me."

"You said you found this outside?" It was Kennedy who spoke now, standing at the back of the couch. She slowly crawled over it, sitting propped up on the back with her feet on the seats. "Where?"

"Down my street," Danny said, "just in the gutter," and then he told them everything about that morning, all about how he could barely get through the day, he was thinking about the game so much. "It's unfinished, though. Look." He loaded in, and walked them through the virtual world, showed them unfinished enemies, text boxes without any text in them, rooms in the digital manor that should've had walls or doors, but their character was instead impeded by an invisible force.

"Whoa," Jason said, long and slow, drawing the word out. "You get this from one of the guys at the Blockbuster?"

"I found it outside," Danny said.

"I've seen demo discs before, but I've never seen an actual unfinished game."

"You wanna play?" Danny asked.

"Hell yeah," Jason said, snatching the controller back. "Same rules as usual?"

"Same rules," Danny said. Then, to Kennedy, "You in?"

"W-we were supposed to go to the party," she said, looking flummoxed at having been asked.

"This is way cooler," Jason said, already wandering through the manor. "Let's do this instead. At least for a little while."

"What are the rules?" Kennedy asked as Jason wandered into a hallway and was promptly rushed by a pixelated monster. After a brief loading screen, he wound up back in the bathroom.

"Shit," he said, and held up the controller in one

hand, resting his head in the other, embarrassed at his immediate failure.

"You die, you pass the controller," Danny said, taking it from Jason.

Kennedy smiled.

"I'm in."

They passed the time like that for a while, each of them making a small amount of progress before they were virtually killed and sent back to their last checkpoint. They dodged monsters and solved puzzles that didn't seem like they should exist inside an actual house that human beings were supposed to live in, but that didn't matter because they were having fun. Danny turned the lights down and they played lit by the glow of only the television and a set of Halloween-orange string lights that draped around the room. They collected items like a compass that only ever pointed north, and a mace—or maul, according to Jason—from an old knight statue. They found an old ring and different keys in the shapes of different animals that unlocked doors with those animals as knockers, unclogged drains that made flooded areas accessible, opened up the basement, discovered secrets hidden in old paintings and revealed the mystery in the game's story.

But beneath it there was something else. Among all the notes and treasures they discovered, all the journal entries and graffiti scribbled onto the walls and cryptic puzzles, Danny perked up at the mention of a House, always capitalized. From the story they put together, the player was in this manor searching for their uncle, a painter, who seemed to have gone insane, and certainly disappeared, driven to madness by the apparition of a House. Their objective as players was to find the House that drove their uncle mad.

"Holy shit," Danny said, and simply let one of the pixelated monsters kill him as the realization slammed into his head.

Kennedy took the controller from him, knowing it was her turn next, but didn't start playing. She noticed the ease with which she'd pulled it from Danny, saw the slack-jawed expression on his face.

"Are you alright?"

"Guys," Danny gasped, remembering the very first note in the game.

Solve the riddle, find the house.

"Guys, I think this game is telling us how to find Gorman's House."

"What?" Jason asked, clearly brushing it off.

"I'm serious!" Danny looked at them and forced himself to slow down as he talked so his mouth didn't outpace his brain. "It's supposed to be a secret attraction, right? They wouldn't just print out flyers and stick them around town. What if this is it? What if this is how we find the House?"

"Isn't that kind of cost-prohibitive?" Kennedy asked, but Danny could see a spark in her eyes.

"All they'd have to do is make it once," Danny said, "and then just print it over and over again. Besides, don't you feel like we're getting to the end?"

It was true. The pacing was ramping up. They were very near to unlocking the attic, the supposed final room of the House.

"What if we get to the end and it tells us where Gorman's House the attraction is? The real House." Danny didn't know what referring to something as a proper noun felt like in his mouth, how it sounded to his ear, but he certainly knew this was it. He watched Kennedy's face light up, saw Jason follow them a little slower, but still come to the same conclusion.

"How much prize money is supposed to be at the end of the House?" Jason asked.

"Depends on the legend," Danny said.

They dove back in.

They avoided enemies and solved new puzzles and opened the attic door with a crow-shaped key and found a large, empty room with a single painting in the middle of the room, still on the easel.

"What is it?" Jason asked as Kennedy held the controller.

Kennedy read aloud, "'Follow the compass, and then seek the knight.'"

"North," Danny said. "Go north, as far north as you can go."

She did, avoiding monsters along the way, keeping hold of the controller, living longer than either Danny or Jason ever had. The northernmost point on the map was a field behind the manor. The field was completely empty, not a single other item in it, only a misty barrier that kept them from continuing.

"The hell is this?" Jason asked, leaning back into the couch.

"Follow the compass," Kennedy recited aloud, "and then seek the knight. There's no knight here."

Danny actually stood up.

"But we have something from the knight."

Kennedy actually gasped.

"The mace."

Then it was Jason's turn.

"The maul."

North. Field. Maul.

They knew where Gorman's House was.

Chapter Four
Gorman's House

The Northfield Mall rested on Beacon's north-ernmost edge, the massive structure a shadow of its former self. It used to be the kind of place where the generations before Danny, Kennedy, and Jason hung out. Not quite old enough for their parents, but their older brothers and sisters certainly. Since the mall's high time in the 80s, the 90s had brought in superstores like Target, Wal-Mart, MacReady's, and all nearer to the center of town. Northfield quickly became obsolete. A few of its stores were still open, but it was far from its former neon-lit glory.

"You sure this is it?" Jason asked as he drove around the mall through weed-choked parking lot after weed-choked parking lot. Most of the lot lights were out, and the entrances into the building itself at the Sears and the Macy's had been covered with newspaper and heavy bolt locks. It didn't look like a place that would've held a secret invite-only haunted house. It looked like a place that ought to be demolished. But maybe that was exactly what made it perfect to do so.

"I'm tellin' you," Danny said from the backseat, "the mall's the answer." He was absolutely sure the solution had been correct. What were the odds they found *Northfield Mall* as an answer and it meant something else?

Kennedy said "There!" and pointed. Half a dozen other cars were all parked near the mall's Lowes home store entrance. There were even a couple bicycles pushed up into the racks or lolled over into the bushes.

"Well, hell, let's go!" Jason sped up through the parking lot, taking the closest spot to the building he could find. "We better hope that prize money ain't all gone by the time we get there!"

Danny had never been inside a dead mall before, had never been in a space meant to hold so many people that was so completely devoid of them. There was something about that absence that didn't feel right. He knew that sometimes kids from Beacon dared one another to break into Northfield after it closed, but he wasn't part of those cliques. The empty vastness was a new experience for him. And judging by the looks on Kennedy's and Jason's faces, it was a new experience for them too. He saw Jason look around, his eyes widening and fingers flexing. Kennedy patted the outside of her thighs repeatedly.

There were other people around them, but it wasn't enough to fill the negative space, mostly kids or teenagers around their own age. A couple kids who looked like they might've gone to the community college. Almost everyone was in costume. Danny saw a handful of Ghostfaces, a sexy Raggedy Ann, a Batman and a Joker with a Penguin who appeared to be someone's little brother, all the girls from *The Craft*, a few Power Rangers, various *Dragon Ball Z* characters. Many of them turned around as Danny's group entered, looking at them quizzically for a moment, seemingly judging that they were explorers as well, searchers for the House and not part of the experience, before ignoring them, and turning back the way they'd been looking.

Back to the center of the mall.

Back to the food court.

Back to Gorman's House.

All the tables and chairs had been removed from the food court, and in their place was a house. Not some flimsy, hastily-assembled structure meant as a lawn decoration, but an actual full-sized *house* in the middle of the mall. A house *inside* was a strange sight and hit Danny in that same uncomfortable, uncanny place where being inside an empty mall hit him. The place where images of mannequins and porcelain dolls lived. A building inside of a building was wrong in a way he couldn't articulate. The structure was so big, Danny first wondered how they were able to get it inside (Piece by piece, like assembling furniture?), and then how it was able to fit at all. The food court and balconies around it seemed to distort, to warp like the images in a kaleidoscope, as if the building was intentionally making room for the house, afraid to touch it.

Danny didn't know anything about house styles, but he knew what this house reminded him of. Old gothic manors, rain-wet and lightning-lit. It looked like that combination of practical sets and matte-painted backgrounds from old movies, as if some parts of the house, like the upper floor and the turrets, were not actually part of the structure of the house itself, but the world around and behind it. The house was tall, but it was also wide, stretching up for three whole stories, higher even than the second floor of the mall, the big glass atrium retreating higher into the air, making room for the house's third floor and the sharp turrets that stuck up from the roof.

For a moment, after looking upon the house, Danny wanted to leave more than anything in the world. There wasn't just an eerie feeling about it, not just something minorly unsettling, but a terror, deep and real, that told him to run, run for the hills. But just like his other real fears, Coach taking in a deep breath to start yelling at the smallest infraction, administrators standing in the doorway to his classroom, the sight of the student resource officer's squad car, that fear left. It was there and then gone, because Danny told himself the danger he was anticipating was not real. It was only the illusion of danger. And even if the danger was real, he was paying attention, had his wits about him, because, as a black boy, he needed to at all times. There was no need to run. It was the same kind of fear he had before he got onto a roller coaster.

But in less than an hour, he'd be telling himself he should've listened to that voice, he should've run.

They all should've run.

The dark presence shuddered with anticipation, but no one could see it. It was a shudder of pleasure so deep that it wasn't reverberated in its physical presence, the wood and plaster of the house that sat in the Northfield Mall, but in its very soul. In the part of it that was in another faraway place. The dark presence shuddered with pleasure, because it knew it was about to feast.

"This may sound like a dumb thing to ask now that we're already here," Jason said as they waited in line, "but who's Gorman?"

Danny and Kennedy turned to look at him. They'd gathered with the rest of the costumed attendants, naturally forming a line that led up to the front of Gorman's House despite the absence of any employee ... or presence at all, really. The house was silent, looming over them as they waited. Maybe this was part of the show. Leave people to stew, get their imaginations going.

"What?" Danny asked. He hadn't really been paying attention. He'd been staring at the house, trying to see if he could see anything through the windows, but the drapes were all drawn.

"Gorman's House," Jason said. "Whose house is this? You know, in the legend."

Danny searched his memory banks, but he didn't know. Gorman's House, Chimera House, the 13th Floor House, he'd never thought of the origins of the names. They were creepy and evocative, and in that way they did their jobs. Now that he thought about it, there weren't a lot of proper nouns in urban legends, period. The babysitter nor the man upstairs ever had names. The man under the car or the killer with the hook hand were always anonymous. Danny had no idea who owned the choking doberman or the identity of anyone involved with the Bunny Man. Places, sometimes. Entities, occasionally. But they often operated by the same set of rules; creepy and evocative. The name Gorman meant nothing to him overtly, even though for some reason, in connection with a haunted house, it always made him think of a mad butcher or killer. He couldn't explain why, there was nothing that explicitly put that thought in his head, it was just what he'd dreamed up.

"I dunno," Danny said, shrugging, "who's Bloody Mary?"

He didn't mean it as a rebuttal, as a way to brush Jason off, but he seemed to take it that way, giving him a sideways look. Danny let it slide. He didn't feel like dealing with it here, now, just wanted to have some fun.

"It might not mean anything," Kennedy said in a way Danny could tell meant she was trying to smooth things over. *Things* being whatever was going on between those two.

"Nothing means nothing," Jason said, leaning out of line and looking up towards the house. "Everything means something." He said that last bit over his shoulder. At Kennedy. At her costume.

Danny didn't know why that was when he'd had enough.

"What is your deal, man?" he asked, stepping ahead so he could face Jason. Others in the line ahead of them shuffled away without making it look like they were deliberately shuffling away. He could see their fear and told himself to bottle his anger, but it just wasn't happening. Danny could feel anger leaking out of his ears like cartoon steam, just like when Coach had grabbed him. But this time he could do something with that anger. "Why are you gunnin' for everybody?"

"I'm not–" and here Jason launched into a poor impersonation of Danny, "*gunnin'* for anybody. Y'all need to stop being so sensitive."

Danny stepped closer, but he didn't touch Jason. He knew what would happen if he put hands on him at all, let alone first; he'd be blamed for the fight. *Green!* Regardless of its actual origin. Regardless of anything. Danny would be blamed because he was ... well, *him*.

"Why are you so up Ken's ass? Just because she didn't wear what you wanted her to?"

"That's not what this is about," Jason said, but his face, suddenly as red as his hair, betrayed him. For Jason, Kennedy was exactly what this was about. But for Danny it wasn't. *Green!* He could feel that anger rolling out of him. Misplaced, meant for Coach, for the unfairness of the world itself, but coming for Jason nonetheless.

Kennedy pushed herself in between the two of them.

"Stop," she said. Just once. Calmly. But it was enough to diffuse the tension. She looked at Danny. "I appreciate it, but I can take care of myself."

Danny felt himself blush. Before he could say anything, Kennedy turned to Jason. "And you." For a moment it seemed like she was going to say more, like she was really going to tear into him, but then she seemed to remember they were in public, that there were other people around, and she simply said, "Play nice."

Jason opened his mouth, but before he could offer any rebuttal, the front door to the House opened.

It moved on hinges so rusted and so loud their screaming sounded like the shrieks of the dying and un-dead. Not only did Danny and Jason step away from one another at the noise, but everyone in line took a hearty step back as the door screeched all the way open.

There was no one there. Just the yawning, black maw of the House.

"What do we do?" asked a Batman from near the front of the line. "Do we ... go inside?" He took a tentative step closer, but didn't go quite so far as to step up onto the porch. Everyone stood there for a long time.

No one came out of the House, and it was impossible to see anything through the dark inside.

"Man," Danny glanced at Jason. "Screw this." He walked away from him, from the whole confrontation, determined to not take that bad energy into the House with him. He walked around the line of costumed people, past the Power Ranger and the Ghostface and the Batman, and into the darkness of the House.

Kennedy had one brief, positive thought in the middle of the confrontation with Jason, but it was immediately supplanted by the inexplicable shudder of true fear she got watching the darkness swallow Danny. Why did she think of it that way? Swallow? And why couldn't she find that happy thought again? It was like the House was some giant, hungry thing, with not just Danny, but her own thoughts as things to be consumed. Kennedy might've called out for Danny, but her fear also might've eaten her voice completely, swallowed it before she had a chance to speak up.

What was that happy thought, and where had it

gone? Into the House? Into that dark entryway?

After Danny went in, the others followed. Batman, the Joker, Ghostface, Jason Voorhees, the Power Ranger, every one of them headed up the porch steps and into the darkness of the House. Even Jason, dressed as Rick O'Connell, followed. He looked over his shoulder, making sure Kennedy was still behind him as he moved.

But she didn't want to follow. She wanted to turn and run, leave this whole adventure behind, even though she knew she couldn't with Danny still inside the House, in its darkness.

It made her want to return to the safety and surety of her Evie Carnahan costume.

Why did she suddenly feel this way? So suddenly feel small?

"You coming?" Jason asked.

Kennedy was very aware of the feel of her Tank Girl costume against her body, of the stockings and the boots and the vest, the bracelets and the socks on her arms. It was the attire of someone who was prepared for a fight, who was ready to take on the big, bad, evil overlords in the post-apocalyptic future. It made Kennedy feel like there was a fight ahead of her, but she didn't want to fight this thing, this House. Looking into the darkness beyond its open door, it made her think there could be no winning, that there was just something too massive about this place, this space. Something so big she stood no chance against, like trying to fight a hurricane.

The Evie costume, on the other hand, even the thought of it, made her feel different. It made her feel like she didn't have to fight, like she would be scared, but there would be someone there to protect her. Jason? Was it him? Was he really the protector he thought himself to be? And was Kennedy really the kind of girl who wanted to be protected, who wanted to sit back and let someone else put themselves on the line?

She thought of Ryan, gliding up to her on her skateboard.

No she was not.

That happy thought, that once-fleeting feeling, sprung up again in Kennedy's chest and she held onto it, keeping it just for herself, a lantern against the darkness.

"I'm coming," she said, not taking Jason's proffered hand, but walking in herself.

Chapter Five
House House

Danny was still steaming. Steaming so bad he forgot he was supposed to be having fun. But then his whole reason for being there dawned on him again as the darkness around him bled away, and he found himself in the first room of the House. It was a small mudroom, a bench to his left, coat rack to his right, and a second interior door right in front of him. There was a large window in the upper half of that door, and though Danny could see a soft, yellow light on the other side, he could not see entirely through the frosted glass.

A shadow moved on the other side of that glass, and a sudden chill ran through Danny he quite enjoyed, one that pushed away the thoughts of stupid Jason and whatever bug was up his butt today, of Coach and Dr. Gunn and the test he promised he'd come back to take again. Yes, this was it, this feeling. The scary fun. Like being on a roller coaster. A safe kind of danger. Danny could still feel his heart beating quickly, but now it was for a reason he actually wanted to nurture, not suppress. He thought about how cool the entire thing was; he'd found a mysterious, unmarked video game cartridge, solved a puzzle inside, which led him to a closed-down mall where he was about to enter a legendary haunted house.

How *cool* was that?

Danny walked tentatively closer to that second interior door, watching the shadow on the other side, but just before he grabbed the handle, the front door burst open and Jason and Kennedy hurried in behind him.

"There you are," Kennedy said. "Are you alright?"

"Hell yeah, I'm alright," Danny said with a bright smile. He wasn't going to let anything else crush this vibe. Not even Jason. But then he saw the look on Kennedy's face, a moment of real fear. "Why wouldn't I be alright?"

She seemed to retreat into herself, as if she had been about to say something she realized sounded foolish.

"Nothing," she said, and then smiled, but it looked forced. "Just scared already."

Jason and Kennedy scanned the small mudroom and Danny followed their eyes to the interior door. He looked back over his shoulder again just as the shadow darted out of sight. Another chill ran through him and he smiled again. Damn, this was cool.

"Well," Jason said, looking at Danny's hand, still hanging out in the open just before the knob, "what are we waiting for?"

Danny turned back towards the interior door, but then stopped. He looked over his shoulder at his friends, at the door they came in through.

"Is it just you?" he asked.

"What do you mean?" Kennedy replied.

"I mean where's everybody else?"

Kennedy and Jason looked back behind them, as if they too just remembered there'd been more people around. A moment passed, one where they all separately tried to think of some explanation for the crowd's sudden departure.

"It's gotta be a trick door or something," Jason said, with what sounded to Danny like his usual false bravado. "Yeah, like a revolving door. It probably spits people into different areas of the house. You know, so it's more scary if you're alone."

It sounded like as good an explanation as any, and yet also somehow a reach. Danny looked back at the door. He was no architect, but there only seemed to be a normal door there, nowhere to hide stairs or some sort of twisting passage. But then again, magicians did saw people in half onstage, so what did he know?

Stop looking for holes, he told himself. *Stop trying to not have fun.* He thought again of the circumstances that brought him here, of how cool and unique they were, of how this would be a day he remembered for a long, long time, a memory he would revisit again and again, and told himself not to taint it with doubt.

Danny opened the door into the House proper.

Gorman's House was an absolute smorgasbord of horrific delights that made the three of them cling to one another in fear and excitement as they passed from room to room. There was no rhyme or reason to their direction through the House, no clearly de-marcated path presented to them like there often was at other haunted attractions. They simply pushed their way through, sometimes lingering in a room, some-times rushing through, sometimes doubling back because what was in a previous room was simply so cool it had to be revisited, or because they'd gotten turned around amidst all the frights. It seemed like whoever designed the architecture of the place made it to be intentionally confusing, like they didn't want it laid out like a normal house.

And in every room they saw some new and delightful horror. The walls of various hallways bent and warped, faces moving behind the plaster, arms reaching out to swipe at, but never actually touch, passersby. An eye peered out at them from behind an ajar door, its unseen owner yanking the door shut as they walked by. They opened it, looked inside, and found a woman drowned in an overflowed bathtub. The word "erase" was written in lipstick on the bathroom mirror. They stepped closer, looking over the tub just as the woman leapt to sudden life and lunged for them through a spray of water and they all ran screaming and laughing from the bathroom.

In the kitchen, a cannibal family served up dinner, a father, son, and daughter sitting at the table while the mother slaved over the bloody stove, ripe with the copper-wet stench of blood and cooking meat. The cannibal kids held their utensils in their hands and the father tucked his napkin into his shirt as the mother turned around, a human foot on a skillet, to ask their guests if they would be joining them for dinner. The children looked at Danny, Kennedy, and Jason with hungry eyes, and they quickly darted out of the kitchen as the family began standing from their chairs.

They climbed the stairs to the upper floors, passing a blood splatter on the wall at the bend. They opened the first door they saw and came upon a child's bedroom, where a long, spindly arm slithered out from under the bed, reaching for them as they stood in the doorway. They slammed the door with fake-frightened screams and continued their journey.

They found a library filled with hundreds of books, dozens of different haunted tomes from myth and legend. The *Necronomicon*, The King in Yellow, *The Mysteries of the Wyrm*. Danny even recognized the *Dux ad Ignotus*, the Guide to the Unknown. Taxidermied animals from owls, foxes, and even the Giant Rat of Sumatra loomed on the walls above them. A ladder came rolling towards them from down a darkened aisle, and slowly every book in the library began shaking, flapping its withered pages in an attempt to fly off the shelves.

When they poked their heads up into the attic, something moved around them, something big and lumbering. They couldn't see it in its entirety, but they could see a pair of large, scalloped wings unfold from a dark shape in the back of the attic, backlit by the small window.

They descended a different set of stairs, walking carefully around an ornate mirror that, for whatever reason, did not reflect any of them, or even the house they were in. Instead, the image it showed was of a lovely-looking gated community. But the longer they looked into the reflection, the more twisted things they saw. There was blood in the gutter, lawn furniture spilled in some unknown struggle, a man standing in the middle of a lawn chewing something wet and crimson.

They moved through a living room where they were spotted by a man in a jean jacket with long, stringy hair. He slowly stalked after them, climbing over the couch, watching them as they fled together, herding them down into the flooded basement where a long, serpentine shape sloshed through the thigh-high water. The man in the jean jacket shut the basement door above them, trapping them inside, and they had to play a high-stakes game of "the floor is lava," to get to the other side of the basement and the storm door there, laughing and screaming as they hopped from furniture to furniture.

They were so pulled into the attraction, so deeply invested in the scares, that they didn't realize they still didn't see another soul as they wandered. Not a single repeated face from the line outside.

But while Danny, Kennedy, and Jason darted from room to room, through dark halls and narrow doorways, while they laughed and screamed with fear and glee, there were other, fouler things going on in the deeper, darker parts of the House. The dozen other partygoers, the ones who had been smart enough to solve the riddles of Gorman's House, were not attuned enough to predict the terrible things that happened in its darkness.

And so they went deeper.

Where they were devoured.

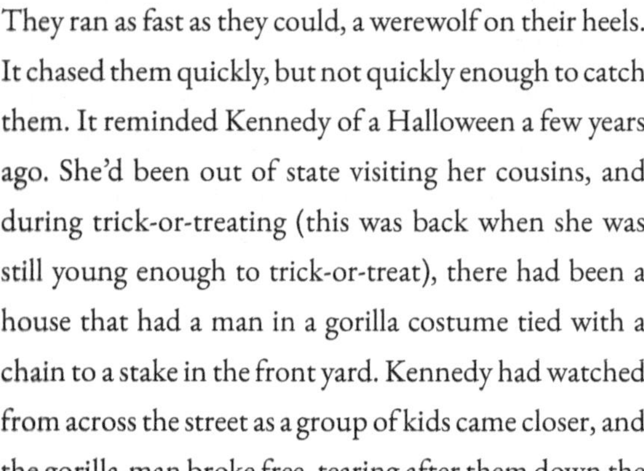

They ran as fast as they could, a werewolf on their heels. It chased them quickly, but not quickly enough to catch them. It reminded Kennedy of a Halloween a few years ago. She'd been out of state visiting her cousins, and during trick-or-treating (this was back when she was still young enough to trick-or-treat), there had been a house that had a man in a gorilla costume tied with a chain to a stake in the front yard. Kennedy had watched from across the street as a group of kids came closer, and the gorilla-man broke free, tearing after them down the street. The werewolf was like that; chasing them enough to make them run, but not enough to catch them.

Kennedy should have felt excitement. She should have felt fun. She should have felt all the same things Danny convinced himself to feel as they entered the house; they had solved an esoteric mystery, had discovered a roaming haunted house, a legend come to life, and were now part of some secret game they'd very likely remember for the rest of their lives, a perfect memory of childhood frozen in amber.

But there was something gnawing at her.

She thought about it as they ran, rolled it around in her head more as the beast gave up the chase and allowed the kids to slow.

Something wasn't right.

"Holy shit," Jason panted, leaning up against a wall in one of the house's nondescript hallways. They'd lost the werewolf around the side of the house, sneaking in through the first side door they saw, huddling low. The exterior door behind them, a hallway that ended in an L-bend in front of them. "I don't know," he panted to Danny, "how you do all this running. I gotta work on my cardio." Jason and Danny ribbed one another, and for a moment it was like it was when things were good. They were all together, all having fun, the only thing that mattered was catching their breath after the running and the raucous laughter.

But Kennedy could just not. Shake. The feeling.

"You alright?"

She looked up from staring at the floor beneath her feet. Danny was looking at her. He too was out of breath, hands on his knees, but he still stood above her. "Too much?"

"No, I ..." It wasn't that, but she didn't know what it was. She couldn't put it to words. Something was just wrong. Like she'd forgotten something. Like some kind of bad deja vu. She imagined this was how dogs were said to feel before thunderstorms.

"It's all fake," Jason said. "It's just makeup and costumes."

"It's not that," Kennedy said, and the way he'd spoken to her made her not want to talk about it anymore.

"Then what is it?" Danny asked. His voice had much more kindness. It told her that it was okay if she needed time to answer, that it was okay if she didn't know at all. She didn't think she did. Or maybe some deep part of her, some primal part, knew, and her higher brain didn't want to face it.

Kennedy raised her head and looked around. There was a small window in the door through which they came and she walked back over to it. Danny and Jason followed her.

"Where are we?" she asked as she stopped before the door. It looked out onto the yard where they'd encountered the werewolf. The beast was no longer there, but Kennedy saw the same turf laid across the floor, cheap, plastic stuff like at putt-putt courses. A neighborhood was painted onto a large backdrop on the other side of a waist-high picket fence, making the place look like an old-timey movie set. She'd seen that as they were running, realized it must've been hidden behind the House's bulk, which was why they didn't see it as they entered. Or maybe someone raised it after all the people went inside. This whole of Gorman's House seemed to function on hidden operators.

"What do you mean?" Danny asked, looking out the window beside her.

The realization hit Kennedy like a ton of bricks. It hit her so hard and so fast her rational mind couldn't keep up with it. She forced herself to slow down, to ask questions while she reviewed her findings again, just to make sure she wasn't wrong.

"Tell me where we are," she said. "I mean, where are we right now? Within the mall."

"I don't understand," Danny said, but the way he said it, the way he looked at her, told her he was beginning to.

"The House is in the food court," Kennedy said. "Where have we been? How far have we run?" She could see Danny and Jason working it over in their own heads. Some of it made sense, Kennedy thought. The first few rooms. The entryway. The kitchen. The bathroom, even. Those all fit within the confines of the borders that were established when they looked at the House from the outside. But somewhere along the way they had become lost. Unmoored. The layout of the House had stopped making sense, and she hadn't noticed because she'd been having too much fun.

Danny said, "How is there a basement?" and she knew he understood. He went on, "How did they make a basement to the House in the middle of the food court?" When she looked at him, he was pale. She could see understanding behind his eyes. It wasn't just the basement.

"You know where we are right now?" Kennedy asked. "Or where we should be?" She thought she knew, but she wanted to know if someone else had come to the same conclusion. Danny looked into the middle distance, and she could tell he was calculating, retracing their steps in the same way she had. She looked over her shoulder and saw Jason doing the exact same thing. The two football players, with field and spatial awareness, came to the same conclusion at the same time.

"Auntie Anne's."

"We *should* be," Kennedy said, looking out the window, "but we're not."

Jason joined them at the door, saying, "Hang on."

He opened it and walked back out into the yard, heedless of the potential werewolf. Kennedy followed him, and Danny behind her. They walked out onto the turf lawn and looked around the space. They saw the painted backgrounds they'd briefly admired when they were running from the werewolf, but they were so distracted they didn't even take in the size, the impossibility of it all.

"There's not enough room for this," Jason said, more to himself than anyone else. And he was right. They should have been standing in the middle of Auntie Anne's right now, back in the employee area, which was crowded with counter space and pretzel confections. "How did they *do* this?" Jason asked, but no one answered. They looked around, realized that whoever made Gorman's House would've had to knock down walls and take out ovens, sinks, countertops, fridges, to make the place where they stood. This outside space was too big. Far too big to make any kind of sense.

"Baskin Robbins should be there," Danny said, pointing to a vastly empty space in the backyard.

"Panda Express," Kennedy pointed with her chin to the side yard. And then, above her, "There should be a balcony here. And over there." She pointed to the other side of the House.

"Wait," Jason said with a small chuckle, "wait, wait, wait, this is just some kind of mistake." But his voice was getting higher, faster. He was trying to convince himself just as much as the others.

But before anyone could say anything else, Danny was moving. He crossed the yard with a purpose, and Kennedy and Jason quickly followed him.

"Where are you going?" Kennedy asked, but they all stopped when they got to the corner of the House. Danny looked around the corner, and when Kennedy and Jason followed his gaze, they only saw more House, more turf yard, more painted neighborhood, all taking up the space where the Burger King and the other big food chains should be.

"Nah, man, this is wrong," Danny said. His hands were in fists at his sides.

Kennedy had her arms around herself, rubbing her shoulders.

"That's the understatement of the year."

Danny turned around and looked at his friends.

"Let's get outta here." He made to move towards the front of the House, but something sailed through the yard, something small and fast. Danny and Kennedy looked back to where Jason stood and found him bent over, arm forward. Danny recognized the stance as Jason's post-throw. He and Kennedy followed Jason's eye-line across the yard, toward the painted neighborhood, which now bore a small hole in it.

"I'm done with this House," he said, not even looking at them. "We're going straight through." Jason walked over to the small hole in the backdrop and stuck his fingers in it. It was thick canvas, and it took him a moment and some help from Danny to rip a hole in it big enough for any of them to fit through. As they tore at it, Kennedy realized she wasn't watching them, but their backs, the rest of the yard, knew she was anticipating something sneaking up on them, some monstrous form far more realistic than the rubber-suited werewolf that had pursued them lumbering through the yard. She pleaded for them to hurry, and once they were finally through, they all took a step back, all struck silent at what was on the other side. There was no familiar mall tile, not even an employees-only back room.

Only a long, bare, hallway with hardwood floors and white walls, ending in an L-bend.

Like what would be found in a House.

"No," Jason said. "No, no, no, no, no," as if he could dispel the strange appearance before them. Kennedy took a step back, away from the painted neighborhood and the impossible hallway behind it. Danny just stood there in silence.

This didn't make sense. Danny was absolutely sure of where they were. This hallway, this L-bent thing that shouldn't be here, should have been the rear of Auntie Anne's. That hall should be leading back into the inner workings of the mall, not deeper into...whatever darkness those four walls led. Danny couldn't take his eyes off the hallway. Some instinct, some vestigial impulse, told him to stay away from that place at all costs. It wasn't lost on him how the single light fixture hanging from the hall ceiling acted as a uvula, making the hall look like a long, dark throat, except for that sudden shift to the right. He blinked quickly, but he could have sworn he saw the hall pulse.

Like it was swallowing.

"Okay!" Jason suddenly said, loudly, "I think I speak for all of us when I say I'm ready to go."

"Yeah," Danny said, not taking his eyes off the hall-way. Kennedy nodded, silently agreeing.

"Hey!" Jason shouted, raising his hands, palms out, a surrender gesture. He lifted his head toward the painted sky. "That's enough, we've had enough fun, but we're ready to go now."

"What are you doing?" Kennedy asked.

Jason said, "They've gotta be watching us. I don't see any cameras, but they gotta be there. Haunted attractions always watch the people inside," he said as he moved around the yard, looking up into the drawn sky and waving his hands. "We don't even care about the prize money, we're ready to leave. You can have somebody in one of those reflective jackets come and take us out now."

But no one came. There was no movement except the creaks and rumbles of a settling House.

Kennedy said, "I don't see any cameras."

Something inside Danny told him he shouldn't, that he needed to keep his eyes on the hall in the same way an antelope needed to keep an eye on what might be a lion in the grass, but he looked away and confirmed what Kennedy said.

And when he looked back, the hall wasn't empty

anymore.

Someone stood there at the far end, twenty feet away.

It was a woman, or so he assumed. The shape was silhouetted, backlit so he could only see its outline. Danny could see slumped shoulders and a head that was tilted forward. Long hair. A skirt or dress, he couldn't really tell, that ended just past the woman's knees. She took a single, fumbling step forward, and then had to reach out and brace herself against the wall.

"Y'all," Danny said, his voice coming out as much more of a harsh whisper than he intended. Kennedy yelped and slapped her hands over her mouth. He was sure he heard Jason audibly swallow.

The woman just stood there, leaning against the wall. Not moving.

"Are you with the House?" Jason asked, stepping closer, but not out of the yard, not into the hall. "Can you take us out of here?"

The woman said nothing.

Jason asked, "Are you hurt?"

The woman shuddered like she wanted to step forward, but held her place against the wall. Jason moved to head to her, but Danny stepped out and grabbed him by the arm.

"What are you doing?" Jason asked.

Danny shook his head. "This ain't right." He looked briefly from Jason to the woman. "Something about this ain't right."

"Danny's right, J," Kennedy said. She came a little closer, sure to keep Jason and the hallway and the woman in her view the entire time. "I don't like this."

Jason scoffed at both of them, but Danny could tell he was really considering it. Danny knew Jason's brain, the brain of a white boy, didn't function the same as a girl's brain or a black boy's brain. It wasn't aware of the same dangers, thought it was on another plane of immortality entirely separate from the average teenager. And yet Danny and Kennedy seemed to be the voices of reason for him. Jason looked away from them and down the hall to the woman, where she still hadn't moved.

"Say something," Jason called to her. "Can you let us know if you're hurt?"

The silhouetted woman took another half-step forward, using the wall for support.

"J, man," Danny said, tightening his grip on Jason's shoulder, "let's split. We head straight back the way we came. Just follow our tracks."

The woman took another step.

But Jason just couldn't let it go.

He shrugged out of Danny's and Kennedy's grip, and when Danny made to follow him, it was Kennedy's turn to grab him by the elbow. Danny looked over his shoulder and saw the conflict in Kennedy's eyes, felt it in the way her fingers tightened and loosened over and over again. She didn't want this, didn't want to be here at all, but she also didn't want Jason in this. She didn't want Danny to put himself in danger, but she also wanted Jason out of it. They were all the same things he was feeling. But in her eyes Danny could see something else, some realization he hadn't come to yet.

"Stay here," Danny said, "I got him."

"No," Kennedy said, not in a rebuttal of what Danny said, but in a denial of everything, the whole situation. "Look at her."

Danny turned back to look just as Jason screamed. It was nothing like the giggly screams of joy they'd been letting loose throughout the night. This was a scream of pure and utter terror, something that reached out from the deepest, most primal part of Jason, a scream that was suddenly and terrifyingly convinced of its own mortality. Just as the woman lunged at Jason, just as the hallway door slammed shut, separating them, Danny saw what she was wearing. What Kennedy was supposed to have been wearing.

She was dressed like Evie Carnahan.

Danny Green was big for a high schooler; nearly six feet and a hundred ninety pounds. He was big in general. And still he could do nothing to budge the thick, oak door that had slammed shut between him and Kennedy and Jason. Danny heard a shout of surprise from Jason just as the door closed, but it was frighteningly silent now. Like that closed door had sequestered Jason off in a completely separate world. Danny backed away, holding the shoulder he was sure he'd bruised from ramming it against the door. He'd seen people do this in movies before, but had no idea if it would really work; he pulled his foot back and kicked at the door, right at the handle, trying to knock it free.

Nothing. It was like it was made of concrete.

"Hey, we give up!" Kennedy called, shouting at the painted neighborhood, at the house, the turf grass and fake bushes, at the ceiling above. "We're finished now, show us the way out!"

But no one answered her.

This was all so incredibly messed up. Danny had no idea how it'd gotten this way, but here they were, trapped in some strange place that shouldn't exist, no help in sight. He turned around and looked at Kennedy.

"We gotta find another way out," he said.

"But ..." she looked over his shoulder at the door, seemingly couldn't bring herself to say it. Neither did Danny want to think about it. He didn't want to think about Jason behind that door, about what it meant that he was now suddenly so quiet. He didn't want to think about it, so of course it was all he could think about.

"I can't get through that door," Danny said. "We gotta try something else."

Kennedy looked like she might fight him on it for a moment, but she took another look at the sturdy door and nodded.

"Come on," Danny said, leading them around the corner of the House, buckets of ice dousing his heart as they went, as they saw more and more. The outside of the House looked exactly the same as they had seen in the food court, the same dark wood, the same three stories, like an old chateau out of a black-and-white horror movie. But gone was the food court and the surrounding mall. That fake, painted neighborhood surrounded them everywhere they went, fencing them in. It was even above them, where the atrium should be, painted sun and clouds.

Danny supposed someone could have thrown all this up after the guests had entered the House. If they had a big enough team and were coordinated enough. But that still didn't explain the spatial impossibilities. It still didn't explain where the second-floor balconies of the mall had gone, where all the stores had vanished to.

"How the hell do we get outta here?" Danny asked as they came upon the front of the House again.

"Retrace our steps?" Kennedy asked. She seemed like she wanted it to come out as a suggestion, but it was more of a question. She looked at Danny, and then away from the House, over her shoulder to the neighborhood that should have been the spot where they'd entered the food court. "Try to cut through the canvas again?"

She offered it just as Danny was thinking it, but he didn't know if he could do it, didn't know if he could face that impossibility once again. He imagined another strong, oak door on the other side of that canvas, another long L-bent hallway, and realized how much of his energy he was using to hold his mind intact. He didn't know how much he had left in him, how much more he could take until he snapped.

He thought the long, harsh creaking sound he heard *was* his mind snapping, slowly popping bit by bit, but he saw Kennedy's eyes widen, saw her look over his shoulder, and realized it was the now-all-too-familiar sound of hinges. Danny whirled and looked towards the House's front porch.

A woman stepped through the threshold and out onto the porch, long, white wedding dress flowing behind her. A veil covered her face so that Danny could see she was white and blond, but not much else. He didn't think she was supposed to be in costume as anyone. No leather jacket, so she couldn't be Tiffany from *Bride of Chucky*. No bandages to mark her as the Bride of Frankenstein. Just an anonymous bride. Which meant she was probably with Gorman's House, and not a visitor; the House didn't have pop culture scares.

The woman waved to them and then beckoned them over.

Danny and Kennedy looked at one another, and then slowly approached the woman, Danny in the lead.

"Hey, you with the House?" he asked.

"Oh, come up, come up, won't you?" the woman said, beckoning them across the lawn, but as they got closer, her demeanor began to change. She tucked her arms into herself just a little more. Through her veil, Danny could see her smile wilt just a little bit. Small changes, microscopic almost. Changes that would have gone unnoticed by anyone except someone like Danny, someone who was attuned to those changes, had been dealing with them his entire life. Changes like women shifting their purses to their other sides as he walked by them on the street. Changes like cashiers watching him as he walked into convenience stores. He wondered if Kennedy noticed those changes too.

"We would like to leave," Danny said, intentionally code-switching. He knew when and how to change the way he talked. Mostly in front of white adults; cops, administrators, sometimes teachers. It made him feel unclean in a way he couldn't entirely define, but he would rather feel dirty than lost in this place one more minute. "Us and our friend too."

He opened his mouth to speak again, but Kennedy was suddenly behind him, suddenly past him, taking two, three of the porch steps, addressing the woman. In the split second in which she passed Danny, their eyes met and something passed from her to him. She knew, he could tell. She had seen the changes in the bride, however small, and she found them just as absurd.

To fear a teenager.

A *child*.

One who was so clearly afraid himself. What kind of person was this woman? What kind of person would feel that towards a kid? The questions lingered over them, even as other ones were answered by Kennedy's approach. Whatever kind of person this woman was, Kennedy would handle her. Kennedy would talk to her. Fade into the background, Danny. Just listen. Just watch. It'll get us out of here faster.

"Our friend got locked behind that door," Kennedy said, gesturing into the side yard. "We all want to leave. We don't care about the prize money or anything. We just wanna go home."

The bride's shoulders slumped.

"Oh, my dear, I'm sorry to hear that."

Closer now, Danny could see a little more through her veil.

See her smile.

It was too big, too wide, like it belonged on a face much larger than hers.

"I'm sorry, but it's far too late for that." The woman reached beside her and touched the doorbell on the side of the house. It rung not with a bell, but with a canned scream, and then the ground opened up underneath Danny and he was falling. He got his arms out just in time to grab the edge of the pit that had opened up beneath him, but it came up too quickly, the ground smashing into his arms, his chest, his chin, and he merely bounced off the lip of the hole and fell into the darkness below, as the bride reached out and grabbed Kennedy, pulling her into the house, that smile on her face now wide and toothy.

Chapter Six
Deepest Fears

K ennedy screamed as the Bride dragged her by the ear into the House. By the *ear*. Like this was a 1950s sitcom and she was a misbehaving daughter. Not like she and her friends were in mortal danger. Not once did Kennedy still think this was part of the experience of the House. Sure, there were plenty of places where haunted attractions were allowed to yell at you, touch you, even hurt you. But not like this. Not against kids.

Whatever this was, it was real.

The Bride pulled her up the porch steps and through the front door, and despite Kennedy hanging onto the Bride's wrist for leverage, it felt like the woman was about to tear the whole side of her face off. The front door slammed behind her, and despite the immediacy of her own situation, she kept thinking about Danny, and what had happened to him. Where he'd gone. The way he'd fallen was simply impossible. Straight through the floor. But nothing they saw here made any sense. Just like what she saw in front of her now didn't make any sense.

Because where she was now was not the same House as before.

She opened her eyes as she fought against the Bride and saw the kitchen was completely different. It looked like this place was made when they were trying to imagine what the future would look like in the 1950s; the refrigerator with the rounded edges, the pastel-colored tiles, the kitchen sink with metal knobs shaped like Xs, not that see-through plastic they had in Kennedy's house. The appliances all had the same pop of candy-coated colors and shiny metal accents like atom-age rocket ships. But there was one thing that caught Kennedy's eye, one thing that, for a moment, made her forget all about the kitchen and the Bride and even Danny and Jason.

A telephone. An actual telephone hanging on the wall.

"Take a seat," the Bride said, throwing Kennedy down into a chair. Even as she hip-checked the metal table edge, she didn't take her eyes off the telephone. She didn't trust this place, didn't want the telephone to disappear during a blink, to have been a figment of her imagination. "Be still," the Bride said, standing over Kennedy, manipulating her limbs as she sat there in the chair. She pushed her knees together, straightened her back, lifted her chin with a sharp-nailed finger. "Sit still like a good girl."

Kennedy opened her mouth to say something—she didn't even know what—but the Bride said "Good girls don't speak unless they're spoken to." This close, Kennedy could see through her veil a bit more clearly, could see to the woman underneath. Or rather what she thought might've been a woman; the proportions were all wrong. It was like looking at someone through frosted glass, their features warped and funhouse-mir-ror-distorted. Eyes too big, mouth with too many yel-low teeth. "Good girls help their mothers get dinner ready, and they do it before Daddy gets home."

A foreign sense of fear drifted through Kennedy then, something that told her she ought to be afraid, she just didn't know why.

"It's very important," the Bride said, rummaging through the kitchen, "that when Daddy gets home, there's a hot meal on the table."

But she was only just beginning to set pots and pans out when Kennedy very clearly heard the front door open and something loud and heavy, with footsteps that shook the whole House, clomp its way inside.

Danny was aware of the impossibility of his fall, aware that the space around him should not have allowed it. He was supposed to be on the tile floor of the food court, not falling through that floor. And yet fall he did. The air rushed past him and his stomach turned as he dropped through complete darkness, fearing a cold, hard floor coming up at him hard and fast. *Something* hit him, but it had give. It had warmth. He slammed down into still water that nevertheless still felt like a ton of bricks. Which certainly hurt, but did not kill him. Danny flailed, righting himself under the surface, before breaching. Wiping the water from his face. Looking around.

More impossible architecture. This space he found himself in should not exist, *could* not exist. And yet it did. Stop trying to figure it out. It was happening whether or not he believed it.

Danny was floating in the pool that was—or maybe should have been—in Beacon High School. There was no way he'd mistake it for anything else. He'd swam in that pool dozens—hundreds of times over the years. He recognized the white tile, the lanes for the swim team separating the general pool area, the deep end on the other side (the pool got as deep as nine, but Danny treaded around the six-foot mark, slowly paddling to where he could stand). He fought against the water-soaked weight of his improvised Harrigan costume and looked around, saw the familiar lifeguard stand, the entrances to the locker rooms. Everything was as he remembered it from school. Except for the windows. There weren't any. There were supposed to be windows right on the other side of the pool, looking not to the outside, but to a hallway that led down to the gymnasium on one side, and the rest of the school on the other.

And then, right as Danny reached the ladder on the side of the pool, he noticed the signs. They were wrong. Oh, man, they were so *wrong*. The one that was supposed to say NO RUNNING read instead YOU CAN'T RUN. There was supposed to be a symbol of a little guy, speed lines around him to show he was running, the red circle-and-slash through him. Instead, the little figure cowered, as if stricken still by fear. The sign that normally said LIFEGUARD MUST BE ON DUTY AT ALL TIMES instead declared YOU ARE BEING WATCHED AT ALL TIMES above a single, red-rimmed eye.

But the ones that were the worst of all were by the entrances to what should be the locker rooms.

There were two, normally. One with the simple universal drawing for MEN, the other for WOMEN. But these two signs said something horrible. Something Danny had only ever heard about from his dad, his grandpa, from Dr. Gunn.

They said WHITES and COLORED.

Slowly, eyes watching every corner of the room, Danny climbed the ladder up and out of the pool. He kept his head on a swivel as he kicked off his waterlogged shoes and peeled off his socks, unbuttoned the yellow dress shirt that was now soaked to a dull orange. Barefoot and with a soaked black tee on, he rolled his slacks up to his knees to wring as much water out of them as possible. There was no way he was fully undressing in this place. Whatever it was. Danny stared across the room at the locker room signs. WHITE and COLORED. The hell kinda place was this?

Danny quickly looked around, searching for the familiar exit doors, despite usually heading straight into the locker room from the pool. In the pool he remembered, the one he was used to, there was a door that led out into the hallway. But there were no windows, and also no door. The only other one besides the locker room were the double doors that led to a maintenance area he knew students weren't allowed. The sign that hung above it displayed something besides the usual warning.

COME IN.

You gotta be joking, Danny thought, staring at it.

Which was when he heard the noise from the locker room.

It was the familiar sound of a door swinging open, the noise of team chatter that should have been reassuring. It sounded like it did just after a game, when the Beacon High Buccaneers went piling into the locker room, high on a victory. Danny instinctively stepped towards the noise, but stopped after two steps.

If everything here was different, why should his team be the same?

WHITES. COLORED.

Danny turned around. He tried to move quickly, tried to move quietly, but was still painfully aware of the sound of his bare feet against the tile, the dripping of his slacks.

A voice called out from the locker room "Hit the showers, gentlemen!" and Danny recognized Coach Walter's deep bellow. He looked over his shoulder and saw the shadow stretch across the wall before he saw Coach himself. Coach stepped out into the pool area, whistle dangling down his chest and over his potbelly. He stopped just at the threshold into the pool area and glared over at Danny.

"*Green!*" he called. Again. He *smiled*. But it was something dark. Something *wrong*. It looked like someone else's smile had been pasted to Coach's face; too big, too wide, too many yellowed teeth. It made him look like the woman who had grabbed Jason. Like the bride who had taken Kennedy.

Danny swallowed.

"Coach..." he said hesitantly. But he knew it wasn't really Coach. It was something that looked like him. The Coach-dressed-thing stepped out of the locker room threshold and into the pool area.

"You're not where you're supposed to be, Green," he said, fondling the whistle that dangled from his neck. "You know where you're supposed to be."

Something behind the COLORED door growled.

"I ain't goin' in there," Danny said, moving backward slowly. "You can't make me go in there."

"Maybe *I* can't," said the Coach-thing, "but I got some boys who can." He clutched the whistle in his grip.

"Coach, don't." Though he wasn't sure why he thought he could stop him.

Coach blew the whistle. The noise was long and shrill, and all of a sudden the chatter coming from the locker room stopped. In its place, a new and horrifying sound made itself known. It was the sound of dozens of feet marching in sync, and yet sounding like they were carrying something. Dragging something. A heavy weight pulled across the floor to the rhythm of the marching feet. Danny saw a shadow against the wall of the threshold, just like he'd seen Coach's. But this thing was not like anything he'd ever seen before. It was not a person, could only be multiple people. A crowd, a mob, all mashed together. All coming for him.

"Boys," Coach called over his shoulder, "get him."

Danny's heart jumped up into his throat when he saw what came around that corner, out of the locker room. At first he thought it was the football team, and in some horrific way he guessed he was right. It was the team, he recognized every player, even in full pads. What he didn't recognize was the way they were put together. At first Danny thought they were all struggling to climb over one another, all fighting to be the first out the door, the first to get to him, the first to fulfill Coach's command, to impress him. But it wasn't that.

God, it was so. Much. Worse than that.

The whole team was glued together somehow, a horrible amalgam of pads and helmets and flailing limbs, as if they'd been fused together as they all slammed into the turf, trying to catch a fumble. There was no blood or stitching where the team members' skin met, but a horrific melding that reminded Danny of the time he accidentally left an action figure on the radiator as a little kid.

The exposed, helmeted heads of his teammates all turned towards him as one, and they wore the same disturbing yellow-toothed smile the bride had, that Coach wore proudly, the smile that announced them all as part of the same horrific whole that haunted Gorman's House. Together, as one terrible mass, the team shouted "*There's no I in team!*"

And they charged after Danny.

Jason heard the door slam shut behind him, and he briefly chanced a look over his shoulder, confirming Danny and Kennedy weren't with him, before turning back to the woman. Maybe it was with the door closed, but the lighting had changed in the hall somehow. He thought the woman was grown at first, someone closer to the age of one of his teachers, and he was half-right; she was older, but she looked like she went to college. Her hair was long and dark and her eyes seemed to reflect that strange nowhere-light that lit the hall, looking up at him as she held onto the wall for balance.

"You alright?" Jason asked. This didn't seem scary. *She* didn't seem scary. Maybe this wasn't part of the Gorman's House scares at all, but some accident, a chance meeting from another attendee. After all, she wasn't in a scary costume like all the other people had been. It took Jason a moment to realize who the woman was dressed as, but when he did, he felt something wriggle in his stomach. She was dressed like Evie Carnahan from *The Mummy*. Like how Kennedy was supposed to be.

"You okay?" he asked again when she didn't respond. The young woman merely held out a hand, beckoning, reaching. "It's all an act," Jason said, walking closer to her. "Just meant to scare you, not hurt you." He had no way of knowing this, not consciously, not without a level of introspection he was not currently capable of, but Jason's entire demeanor changed in the presence of what he perceived to be an injured woman. He stood taller, puffed his chest out more. He pitched his voice lower, but not comically so. He walked directly, with a purpose, right up to her, and held out his hands, palms up in an *I mean you no harm* gesture.

"I'm Jason," he said, like he'd forgotten completely about the revelation he'd just come upon with Danny and Kennedy, because he had. His brain was being overridden. Not by force, but by subterfuge. "Are you alright?"

The woman took his hands, holding onto him for balance. Coming closer.

"We'll get outta here," he said. "They can't keep us in here if we want to go. There has to be some eject clause, right?"

Again, without speaking, the woman nodded. She nervously bit her lip, breathed out a wordless agreement, slowly moving closer to Jason so that she was in his arms, her body against his.

"Just stick with me," Jason said. "I've got friends in here who are trying to get out too. Everything's ... gonna be just ..." but he couldn't continue, didn't finish, because as he spoke, the Evie-Carnahan-dressed woman came closer and closer, to the point where she could come no closer, her stomach pressed tightly against his, her arms snaking up and over his shoulders. Jason felt a small and painful pinch at the back of his neck, but he ignored it, was focused entirely on the face coming closer to his, the soft lips opening, the tongue gently flicking. The woman kissed him, and he felt that twinge at the back of his neck again, harder and more painful, but he again ignored it, because this was what he'd been waiting for all night.

Kennedy held absolutely still as something impossible walked into the kitchen with them. Something that seemed to warp the very air around it. Kennedy could feel a kind of oppression, a weight, press down on her as the figure sauntered into the room. She didn't know if it was real, didn't know if it was even possible, but she thought of the T-rex in *Jurassic Park*, the idea that if she just didn't move, this thing would not be able to see her. She couldn't bear the thought of closing her eyes, so instead picked a spot on the wall above the woman's shoulder and stared at that, a small bubble in the wallpaper that had escaped someone's exacting eye.

Kennedy flinched as the stomping presence entered the room with them, its clomping boots changing to the harsh clack of hard-soled dress shoes on tile, each of its steps like a gunshot as it came closer. She looked at the thing out of her peripheral vision and saw something large and humanoid. The woman beckoned it into the kitchen with an overly-acted "Welcome home, honey!", a gesture that for some reason suddenly made Kennedy unable to resist looking at it.

The thing was a man, or at least shaped like one. He was tall, wore a suit that appeared too clean, too pressed, like it had just come from the dry-cleaners moments ago and he'd avoided any harsh movements in order to not crinkle it.

"Something smells good," he said, still facing away from Kennedy. There was something terribly wrong with his voice. It didn't come from him but seemed projected from every inch of the kitchen itself, like the place was filled with hidden speakers.

"Dinner's almost ready," the woman said. "Why don't you go and sit down."

"Excellent," said the Father Figure, leaving the kitchen without a glance at Kennedy, shrugging out of his suit jacket as he crossed the threshold, shoes popping against the tile, against the hardwood floor, echoes sounding less like gunshots now, and more like breaking bones.

Jason lifted his head out of the huddle, clapped his hands.

"Break!" he shouted with the rest of the team, as they all separated and took up their positions on the line. The black-and-purple Beacon Buccaneers squared up against the silver-and-white-clad players of Berryman High. Jason looked out across the players, the field, the bleachers, and thought everything seemed normal, that this was just like any other game, despite the fact that he could see nothing beyond the field. The parking lot, the school, everything else in the world seemed shrouded by a kind of deep, off-stage darkness. The kind of dark it was impossible to see into when you were in a place that's brightly lit. No, the only thing that bothered Jason, and it was something he only momentarily swatted at before forgetting, was the strange pinch at the back of his neck, like a bug bite.

But he had things to do.

Jason called the play and the center snapped him the ball. He looked out over the field, testing his options. They didn't have far to go, only ten yards, but all his receivers were covered. He faked a hand-off and took the ball in himself, full well knowing he shouldn't, knowing Coach would have something to say about that later like he had something to say to Danny the other day, but it didn't matter when the cheers erupted, when everyone came running over from the sidelines and pouring down from the bleachers to surround him and haul him up into the air, victorious.

A part of Jason thought that final play felt easy, too easy, like someone had cleared the way for him, but he didn't think too much about it. It didn't matter now that everyone was around him, had their hands on him as if trying to catch just a little bit of his greatness. Even that strange, ever-present pinch at the back of his neck felt like it was gone.

But it was still very much there.

Jason woke up, even though he wasn't really sure he'd ever been asleep in the first place. Or maybe he'd finally fallen asleep after being awake for too long? He wasn't really sure. All he was sure of was he didn't want to leave this place. He moved in the same way you do in dreams, suddenly, inexplicably, somewhere else, without a transition. The somewhere else he found himself was on a raised platform in the middle of the school gymnasium. He sat on a throne with a crown on his head and realized he had, in fact, been crowned Homecoming King. He looked down and saw he still wore his Rick O'Connell costume, but the Homecoming Queen's seat, what should have by all accounts been Kennedy's seat, was empty.

Jason looked out at the sea of faces, all his friends, the chaperons on the edges of the crowd. They too, were expectant. Waiting. *Where is she?* all those faces seemed to ask. They couldn't very well get the party started without the Homecoming Queen.

Jason felt that strange twinge at the back of his neck again. He reached up to swat at it, scratch it, whatever, but a hand gently held onto his wrist and stopped him.

Don't worry, said a voice that strangely echoed. It felt like Jason didn't hear it with his ears so much as with his mind, the voice completely bypassing that pesky physicality. He had the briefest desire to turn around, to look in the direction of the voice's owner, but as soon as it flitted into his head, it danced right out as if sucked away on a harsh wind. *It'll only make it worse if you scratch it.*

Must've been poison ivy or something. Jason didn't

want to spread that around, especially not on homecoming night. He lowered his hand, not thinking of looking over his shoulder at the owner of the voice.

"We still need Kennedy," Jason said, his mind already on other things. "We can't start without the queen."

He didn't see it, couldn't see it, but behind him, the owner of the voice gave a familiar, hideous, yellow-toothed smile.

"Listen to me," the woman said, holding Kennedy by the elbow. "You have to do everything I say, do you understand?" There was something strange in the woman's voice Kennedy could not identify now that the Father Figure had arrived. Before, the woman seemed tyrannical, angry, but now, with him in the other room, she seemed almost ... desperate. That emotion bubbled up, but vanished quickly, like a flash of lightning, and when the woman's plastic facade was plastered onto her face again, Kennedy wondered if it was ever there at all.

They walked into the dining room together, carrying

plates of food Kennedy didn't remember picking up at all, and stood before the table. Before the Father Figure. Kennedy looked at the man, at the *thing*, and blinked. She thought for a moment she had something in her eye, some film or dust that made him look the way he did, but, no, it was just him. For a moment, looking across the room at him, Kennedy thought she was looking at her own father. She recognized the graying at his temples, the thin nose, the high cheekbones. But when she looked at him from another angle, he seemed to *shift* in some way, and instead she found herself looking at Mr. Henderson, the father of one of the girls from the cheer squad. She saw his widow's peak and bushy eyebrows, and when she set the plate down in front of the Father Figure he'd changed again to look more like Coach Walter, balding, muscular. She recognized, at a different angle, Ryan's father, Mr. Darnielle, whom she'd only ever seen from a distance, but she could still identify that skinny frame, that near-constant five-o'-clock shadow.

From every angle Kennedy looked at the Father Figure, he shifted into a different man.

She found herself sitting down next to him, on his left-hand side. The woman was directly across from her.

Before each of them was a plate of some horrible-looking undercooked meat. Kennedy refused to pick up a knife and fork, but the Father Figure dug in, cutting off chunks that seemed too big, but somehow he swallowed them, jaw opening wide like a snake's, yellow teeth tearing into the meat.

Something around Kennedy told her to sit still in her chair, to eat, to not ask questions about what was going on. Even the expression on the woman's face said that. But she couldn't. She had to know, had to figure out how she'd ended up in this horrible upside-down place.

"What is this?" she asked, meaning this whole thing. This House. These people. This dinner.

The Father Figure looked up. "You're not going to eat?" he asked, his face shifting into personas Kennedy could not identify. He didn't wait for her to respond before he said "Then you can go to your room." He stood up, and the legs of his chair grinding against the hardwood floor sounded like banshee screams. He grabbed Kennedy by the back of the neck like someone would scruff a dog, and hauled her effortlessly up and out of her seat. The Father Figure's hands were ice-cold, and Kennedy fought futilely against him, but his meaty fingers wrapped almost entirely around her neck. He carried her up the stairs and tossed her through the first doorway. She hit the ground hard and was shunted into complete darkness as the door closed her in.

A spotlight came on from somewhere in the dark. It shined bright, directly into Kennedy's face. She held up her arm to block it, and when she did, she realized her Tank Girl tube sock was gone.

Everything, in fact, was gone.

Kennedy stood taller than she expected, and she realized it was because she was wearing heels. Not the heels of her improvised Tank Girl costume boots, no, but formal, black high heels. Everything about her outfit was different, changed at the snap of a finger. Tank Girl was gone completely, replaced with a simple, elegant black dress that made her feel like a department store mannequin. Her hair was pulled into a bun, yanked tight against her scalp, and Kennedy could feel makeup caked all over her face.

Everything about her attire was different, just as everything about where she stood was different. She was no longer in the House, or so it seemed, but in the wide open space of her school's gymnasium. There were dozens of people milling about the center of the room, all in the same formal attire as her. Kennedy instinctively looked for a way out, for the red EXIT signs that should be hanging above. But not only did she not see them, she saw no doors of any kind.

What is this place?

"Stand up straight," a familiar voice said, and Kennedy felt a twinge on her side as someone pinched her. She turned to face the voice and found the woman from the kitchen standing beside her. She wore a formal dress as well, but hers was still styled with a 1950s aesthetic, wide lapels, a polka-dot pattern. She wore immaculately-white pumps and stockings with the line going straight up the backs of her legs.

"Nobody likes a sloucher," the woman said, moving around Kennedy to fiddle with every inch of her; smooth a crease, adjust a loose hair, straighten her stance. "This is a very important part of the process," the woman continued, pushing Kennedy's head straight ahead so that she looked out into the throng of people. Most of them were gathered in the middle of the large room, paired up and dancing, very wholesome, very mid-tempo, dancing before a raised podium above which was hung a giant banner that read HOMECOMING KING AND QUEEN. Below that banner were two thrones. One was empty.

The other held Jason.

He sat in the throne completely carefree, looking out over the people like he was having the time of his life. The crown of the Homecoming King was placed on his head, and he even held a large scepter. He looked out over the crowd for a moment before his eyes narrowed in on Kennedy, like he knew exactly where she'd be in the room. He raised a hand and waived, and then pointed at her, and in just those two motions his demeanor changed. The wave was a hello, a harmless greeting, but in the point there was something more sinister, the ghost of the thing she saw on his face when he picked her up earlier that night, when he saw she was dressed as Tank Girl and not Evie.

A figure approached out of the crowd, a faceless young man in a suit who looked like an animated mannequin. He strode confidently up to Kennedy and the woman, offered his hand. He didn't actually say anything.

The woman pushed Kennedy's shoulders, shoving

her across the empty space and into the young man's arms.

No, Kennedy thought, suddenly unable to speak. *No, I don't want this. I don't want anything to do with this.* But the young man took hold of her, grabbing her firmly by the wrist and the waist, and danced them off into the crowd together towards Jason, despite Kennedy's voiced protestations.

Something kicked in as Danny ran, circling the pool, keeping the water between him and the enormous, horrendous team-thing. It felt like the same thing that happened to him when he was on the field and the game was really intense, something that muffled his emotions and focused all his energy into his body, into a Terminator-like analysis of the world around him. Coach, that terrible smile on his face, was in front of the locker room doors; he couldn't go that way. His only hope of exit was the door behind him, the one with the COME IN sign. He didn't want to do that, but there wasn't anything in the world he wanted less than to stay there with the team.

So Danny spun on his heel and ran.

That awareness reminded him of the water, of the tile, told him that if he slipped and fell—if he didn't outright crack his skull open—the team would get him. He forced himself to move slower, to not sprint outright, to keep his center of gravity lower. He heard an enormous, thunderous splash and chanced a look over his shoulder.

The team had thrown themselves (*Itself?*) into the pool. Water exploded up and over the tile, hitting the walls, hitting the ceiling as the amalgamation powered through the chlorine water at an insane speed that should not have been possible with such a bulk, with such an awkward assemblage of limbs. Coach ran alongside the team blowing his whistle, seemingly having forgotten about Danny entirely, now acting like he was judging the team's speed.

"Come on, come on, come on!" Coach shouted between whistle bursts, moving across the wet tile with the same crouched speed as Danny. When the team started moving faster, gaining on him, his horrible yellow smile widened.

Danny ran faster, looking at the doors in front of

him, not the sign, not trying to think about what it could mean, thinking only of escape. Behind him, there was another wet explosion, and he didn't need to look over his shoulder to know it must be the team surfacing from the shallow end of the pool, coming for him. Danny threw himself through the door. He had a moment to take in a familiar tiled school hallway, and yet another moment to think *this isn't where I should be* before his instincts took over and he spun around, forcing the door shut behind him.

Through the gap in the double doors, he saw the team rising out of the water. Coach stood at the edge of the pool, pointing at Danny and blowing his whistle until he was red in the face. Danny pushed the door shut and grabbed a chair from a nearby desk that sat in the hall, for once, finally grateful for the school's need to ever-patrol its students. He slipped the legs of the chair over the pry bars and prayed to anyone who would listen that it would hold.

The team slammed into the doors, and hold they did. They strained against the chair legs but did not break them. Danny stepped back, looking up at the massive figure on the other side of the door through the door's two small vertical windows. Faces that looked like his teammates but could not possibly be glared at him through their helmets, staring at him with an intensity that surpassed what was normally reserved for their rivals at Berryman High. Danny knew, looking into those stares, that if they caught him, they would kill him.

Or worse.

Somehow, they would make him one of them. Somehow they would make him become part of their twisted amalgam.

Someone's hand slapped against the window in the door and drew Danny's attention.

"Jason?"

He was there, but it wasn't really him. It couldn't be. Or at least he hoped it wasn't. That woman had grabbed Jason, the woman in the hallway. She wouldn't have had time to ... make him this.

"Hey, there, buddy," Jason said, his voice muffled from the other side of the door. "Why don't you join us?"

Danny was right. It wasn't him. He spoke with that same strange tone, had that same bizarre, yellow-toothed smile, that same wild look in his eyes, that Coach did. It wasn't Jason, but something that wanted to make Danny think it was. And if it wasn't Jason, maybe that meant there was still a chance to save him. Kennedy too.

But only if he saved himself first.

The team shuffled to the side and Coach appeared in one of the windows.

"Go on, Green. Run. We'll catch you."

It felt like an eternity before Danny was comfortable actually turning his back on the door, on the windows, even though Coach and the team had left. He waited, watching those small windows for a long time before he finally turned and looked at the hallway where he found himself.

But he noticed something about himself first; he wasn't soaking wet anymore. In fact, Danny's whole outfit had completely changed. Instead of his home-made Halloween costume, he found himself back in his school clothes; jeans, sneakers, and his letterman jacket. Somehow, he found that even more upsetting than the monstrous team. Clearly, there was something wrong about this space, but its ability to manipulate *him*, not just itself, was wrong on an entirely different level.

Danny clenched his fists and looked up. He couldn't think about that now, had to think about how to get out of here—Correction, how to find Kennedy and Jason, and *then* get the hell out of there. He didn't want to imagine the horrors this place was subjecting them to.

Danny faced down a long, brightly-lit school corridor. Lockers lined the walls, and every couple dozen feet there was a door. The hallway split off to the left and right maybe fifty yards ahead, but it also kept going, down to another pair of double doors. Danny wasn't sure of which way to go, but he knew he wasn't going back, so he started forward. He moved slowly, quietly, grateful now for the sneakers on his feet, wrong as they felt on him. He stayed low as he came to the first door and quietly peered in.

The way things had been going, Danny expected something other than a classroom, but that was what he got, even though it wasn't like any classroom he'd seen before. It was like they looked in old educational films; every single one of the kids paying rapt attention. So rapt, in fact, they didn't notice Danny at all. The teacher asked a muffled question and every single one of the kids raised their hand to offer an answer. Just like in some of Danny's classes, there were only a couple black kids. They all sat in the back of class, together. The teacher nodded her approval after selecting a student and hearing their answer, then turned to the blackboard and scribbled something down.

When she did, Danny saw her face, and that horrible, yellow smile.

Danny darted away from the window and crept to the corner where the two halls met, holding still and quietly peering. He saw nothing but more hallway to the right, but he heard the sound of running footsteps before he even turned to the left. He looked around the corner quickly, knowing there was nowhere to hide, knowing whatever this was, it was coming for him, and he might as well see it before it got to him.

It was a police officer with a bright orange sash around his chest that marked him as a student resource officer.

And he was running full tilt right at Danny. The look on the cop's face was wide-eyed and rabid, like he'd been waiting for this, this exact moment, for *Danny*, for years. He was drooling as he ran, tongue lolling like a dog chasing a ball, hanging out of a yellow, smiling mouth. There was a predatory glee in his eye, not like an animal hunting, but of a killer stalking, of someone who would do their job not because it was a job, but because they enjoyed it more than anything in the world.

"No! Running! In the! Halls!"

But damn straight Danny ran.

He ran faster than he ever had in his life.

Danny burst through the set of double doors at the far end of the hall. He was aware of being in a large room, but before he could even take it in, he grabbed a nearby chair and dropped the legs through the closed double door's pry bars, just like before. He watched with satisfaction as the mad, drooling student resource officer slammed into the doors, but could not open them. He glared at Danny through the glass for a moment before turning and heading off in another direction. Once Danny was sure he was gone, he turned and took in the room.

He was in the Beacon High School gymnasium, or

at least some version of it. Like the pool, little things were different, things Danny might not have noticed had he not been looking out for them. The gym he remembered had small windows up near the tops of the walls. Those were gone. The neon exit signs weren't there anymore, only the door through which he'd come. They were completely closed in, Danny and the strange group of dancers that crowded the gym floor. Some of them were dressed in formal attire, suits and dresses fit for homecoming, but others wore Halloween costumes that matched the aesthetic of the decoration-draped gym. He saw Ghostfaces and Power Rangers, a Superman and a generic sheet-ghost, a Goku and *Goosebumps'* Slappy. It all complemented the pumpkins and the jack-o'-lanterns and the cornucopias and bats.

A small stage had been erected at the back of the gym, onto which they'd put the thrones for homecoming king and queen.

Jason sat on the king's throne. He still had his costume on, but he had the homecoming crown on his head, perfectly adjusted.

"Danny!" he shouted happily, like kids did on Monday mornings after not seeing their friends all weekend. Suddenly, spotlights came on in the rafters above, pointing beams of hot, white light down at him. They blinded Danny for a moment, and he expected a rush, an attack from the throng of costumed dancers, but nothing happened. Jason just kept talking; "Glad you could finally make it!"

The beams of the lights eased up, and Danny could see again. Jason wasn't alone on the stage; Coach stood by him, his hand on his shoulder.

Or, rather, the thing that looked like Coach. There was something about this thing's eyes, its *face*, something that somehow screamed to Danny that it was not human, only pretending to be. He looked at the way it held tight to Jason's shoulder, like it demanded he sit there and not move from that throne. Coach was different from the other strange faces in the crowd, more visceral, more *real*, like they were in black-and-white and he was in color, even though they all had that same yellow-toothed grin.

"Jason," Danny said cautiously, "what's going on, man?" He looked across the sea of faces, trying to discern about Jason the same thing he could about Coach, but Jason was different. He wasn't like that fake Jason Danny had seen earlier, the center of that horrifying team amalgam. This was *Jason*.

"What's going on?" Jason echoed, like he was surprised Danny couldn't figure it out. "It's homecoming! We're all finally here!" Jason gestured into the crowd, and Danny followed the line of his arm.

Kennedy.

One of those mannequin-dancer-things held onto her, held her tight like it was trying to dance with her despite her obvious protestations. She looked through the crowd to Danny, fear apparent on her face. Danny could see, in her eyes too, that this was really Kennedy. She tried to reach out to him, but the dancer pulled her away, closer to the stage. To Jason.

"The king," Jason said, gesturing to his crown, "the queen," to Kennedy, "and the best bud." He nodded to Danny, and then his eyes lowered, his face darkened. "The *traitor*."

Danny tensed, again ready for an attack, but none came. All the dancers continued to stare at him, to keep him on his toes. To let him know the attack he expected was coming, but to not know when.

"What are you talkin' about, man?" Danny asked. Up on stage, the thing that looked like Coach tightened its grip on Jason's shoulder. It leaned over and whispered something into Jason's ear, that mouth moving too much and too fast, taking up too much of his face, and for a moment Danny thought he saw something there in Coach's place. Just a second. Like the flickers of Tyler Durden during *Fight Club*, there for a frame and then gone, too fast for him to even begin to imagine what it was.

"I'm talkin' about you," Jason said, "Danny Green, Beacon High's new favorite player."

"Is that what this is about?" Danny asked. "Are you for real, dude?"

But Jason steamrolled him, talked right over him like he wasn't even there.

"That wasn't enough," he growled. "Then you had to go and take my girl too."

Danny saw the look on Kennedy's face, saw how she very much did not believe she was anybody's girl.

"I don't know what you think is going on," Danny said, "but me and Kennedy ain't a thing." For the briefest of moments he thought about saying he was pretty sure she didn't even like guys, but there was still some civilized, rational part of his brain activated, a part that told him that secret was not his to tell, and so he kept quiet.

"Sure, sure, sure," Jason said in a way that said he

obviously did not believe him. "I'm sure Lancelot said the same thing."

Danny looked at the Coach-thing attached to Jason's shoulder.

"J, man, why don't you step down off that stage. Let's talk this out. You're buggin'."

"Nah," Jason said, leaning back in his throne. "I got a better idea. Let's take this to the field."

The Coach-thing raised its whistle to its lips and blew a single, long, ear-piercing shriek that had Danny covering his ears—

and when he lifted his head, he found himself some-place else, somewhere familiar; the football field at Bea-con High. Or at least that's what it reminded him of. He recognized the bleachers to his left, the school building suddenly—somehow—to his right instead of behind him. The sun was setting behind it, casting the building in silhouette, black before blood-stained orange, like the beginning of *Bram Stoker's Dracula*. There were even people on the hill, coming down from the school toward the field. They moved in a way Danny didn't like, with a strange and loping gait, like they were drunk. Or dead. Like the ghouls in the new *Night of the Living Dead*.

"Huddle up!" someone shouted, and Danny found himself slowing, not running but jogging now, coming to a stop before his team, who had all gathered—separately, not in their terrible amalgamation—on the sidelines. He stopped before Jason, wanted to open his mouth, to say something, to ask if Jason was alright after that woman grabbed him, but he didn't. This person, this thing, it was no more Jason than the thing at the pool had been Coach Walter. Danny could see it in his eyes. They were quite literally the wrong color, brown instead of blue. It almost made him want to buy it, almost made him want to believe, but the subtle difference was there.

"Fourth and long," the Jason-thing said, looking around at the other teammates before stopping on Danny. "We make this, we can win it. It's our last chance, so I'm gonna throw to you, Green." Green. The boys always called one another by their last names whenever they were on the field, whenever they were in football mode. It was strange, Danny thought, how that mask slipped on and off. Jason said, "You gonna make it?" to Danny.

"I'm gonna make it," he said, not knowing why, not knowing how he'd been pulled into this, only that he had, that he had to play along, and then the huddle broke and they were on the line. Jason made the snap. The lines crashed into one another. Danny shook his defender. Running. Running. The ball was in the air for a short throw, and then it was in his hands, and Danny was running again, running some more, as everything around him changed. He watched the sun set behind the image of the school, taking the light with it, leaving only the harsh yellows of the fluorescent field lights. But even those, with the harsh slamming noise of electric breakers, went out one by one. The shapes that were meandering down towards the field became dark blobs in an even darker world, and Danny knew without a shadow of a doubt that they were coming for him. He looked to his left and watched the lights above the bleachers go out, the crowd shunted off into darkness, and he kept running. Behind him, he could hear dozens of trampling feet and, chancing a look over his shoulder, saw he was being pursued not just by the opponents, but by his own team. Everyone hurried after him, running closer together, holding onto one another, molding together as the lights went out above them, leaving him pursued by shadows.

No, no, no, Danny thought, *not again. Not another one.* He faced front, towards the only light left, the ones directly above the endzone, where a long figure stood.

Dr. Gunn.

Even from this distance, somehow, Danny could see his teacher, see that he was *him*, not like the not-Coach, not like the not-Jason. Maybe not Dr. Gunn himself, in the flesh, but at least not a monster. He stood in the endzone and waved Danny forward, urged him on. Here was light. Here was safety.

And he was going to make it. He was so close.

And then someone blindsided him and knocked him to the turf. Danny still had the wind knocked out of him when the team, the horrible mass of limbs, descended on him.

Kennedy tried to free herself from the mannequin-thing's grip, but it was iron. It was like she was locked in handcuffs. The arm around her waist had tightened, gripping her harder. Something had her feet, her ankles, but she was held so close to the monstrosity she could not look down to see what it was. Nevertheless, they spun, wove through the dance floor with practiced ease before passing her up to the stage.

Kennedy looked around, trying and failing to get a true lay of the land with all the spinning and moving. All she could see were the dozens of other pairs of dancers, the heads of chaperons popping up above the suit-and-dress-clad sea. Around them, the music slowed down, the dancers slowed down, and she stopped, facing Jason, who was pulling her closer just as all the other dancers pulled their partners closer.

"King and queen," he said.

"No," Kennedy protested. She knew what Jason wanted. She'd taken Health class. And while she wasn't averse to the thought of physicality, was quite interested in it, actually, she was averse to the thought that it was *owed*, that it was something she *had* to do, and especially had to do with, seemingly, whichever boy asked her. "Jason," she said, pushing on his chest even though he pulled her forward.

"I said *no*!"

Kennedy kneed him in the balls.

Jason grunted and let her go, but just as he screamed, the thing that looked like Coach Walter wailed. She didn't realize until she looked behind Jason that it still had its grip on him, still held him by the back of the neck so tight that its fingers were digging into his skin. It pulled Jason aside and growled at her with that yellow mouth, and then it reached out to grab her too.

Danny felt the horrible rush as air left his lungs, as an insurmountable weight slammed down on him, and he was positive he was going to die right then and there. Crushed to death under the weight of all his monstrous teammates. One by one his pursuers piled atop him, dogpiling him as if he were the fumbled ball, crushing him deeper into the turf. Danny tried to scream, tried to breathe, but every time he stretched and air left his lungs it refused to return. He felt their hands on him, grabbing him, holding him in place.

I'm gonna die here, he thought, trying and failing to crawl out from under the pile of bodies, trapped under the weight, held down by their hands. He was gonna die in this House he'd become strangely obsessed with, in this memory of a place he never really wanted to be. And for what? What was the point of all this? What had he been trying to prove by coming here, by dragging Jason and Kennedy with him? Oh, God—In the immediacy of his fear, he'd nearly forgotten about them. What was happening to them while Danny writhed under this horrible mass? Were they experiencing similar terrors? If they got out—or if they died—what would they think of him? Would this death be one they thought he deserved? Or would anyone ever know he was dead at all, consumed by this horrible House, crushed to death by all the—

Danny realized something. That realization clicked beneath the surface of his brain and his muscles reactivated, pushing against the pile of bodies threatening to crush him. He realized it in a way he couldn't fully articulate yet, a way where he had to consciously walk through the process to confirm that it made sense. Lying on his back in the turf, he strained against the dog-pile, lifting them upward like he would bench-pressing, and as he lifted them, he saw their faces and terrible yellow-mouthed grins, again reaffirming the quick series of connections his brain made. He pushed the mass upward, and he saw Coach in there. Jason, the captain, the leader. They were all authority figures. People with power over Danny. Even the team, in its own, weird way, its existence as one entity, a peer group that became one singular, writhing thing held an authority over him. Danny thought about them all in the van during Mischief Night, thought about Coach, that whistle dangling from around his neck, hollering from the sidelines. He thought about the way teachers looked at him as he sat in the back of class, the way women looked at him when he was on the same side of the street as him and one singular, rising through hurtled its way through his mind.

I'm just a kid.

He didn't want to think it before. No teenager ever wanted to think of it; themself as a child. But that was what they all were. That was what Danny was. Danny, like everyone else his age, wanted to be grown, and he wanted to be treated like he was grown. But he didn't know that treatment would be different than everyone else's. That the world would pound him into a specific shape with a harshness that it spared kids like Jason.

Danny's muscles strained, shaking under the weight

of the bodies. Several of them he could see, could feel, crawling through the tangle of limbs to get to him. They were coming for him. Danny pushed one more time, summoning the last vestiges of his strength, but Coach's arm reached down through the dogpile towards him, grabbed him by the chest, and where his palm touched him, Danny suddenly felt a white-hot burning. He screamed at the top of his lungs, muscles quivering at the pain, but he could not drop the pile. He didn't know what, but he knew something terrible would happen if he did. Danny felt another hot grip against his ankle, his shoulder, hands and nails sinking into him, smelled burning, and when he looked down at Coach's hand, saw that it was searing its way through his shirt, burning his very skin.

No, not just burning.

Melting.

Molding.

Everywhere they touched Danny their skin was becoming fused with his, their fingers sinking into him like damp earth. Danny could see paleness spreading across his chest, like ink dripped into water, and when he looked back up, saw it was not happening only to him. Every person in the dogpile who was touching someone else was melting into them, their forms mashing together like warm wax.

"Get off me!" Danny screamed, pushing at Coach's face, but all he managed to do was shift its right side into a horrible, twisted grin, eye spun around to the side of its head, yellow smile curlicuing up and around his face. Above him, the entire dogpile shifted and warped as its occupants touched one another, shifted into one another, *became* one another. They were one giant, writhing mass with a dozen arms, a hundred eyes, face after face after face and grin after grin after grin.

And they pulled Danny into its mass.

It was dark where he found himself. Wherever that was. It seemed like nowhere. It could have been everywhere. It was dark all around, so dark Danny couldn't tell what was even up and what was down. He floated through darkness, low, uncaring. Something told him he should feel, but ... somehow it just didn't seem important. Danny floated through the dark, passing little pinpricks of light in the distance. Something deep inside him told him to go inspect that light, but he just didn't … care. Only after one drifted closer to him and he found himself looking into it, did he really get to see.

It wasn't a window, wasn't even a shape, really, but he saw through it just the same. Danny saw himself on the football field, running, running, taking the ball in for a touchdown. He scored, and the team cheered, the bleachers erupted. Danny felt something in his chest, something he wasn't entirely sure how to identify, but it left him as the light and its images drifted away.

He passed by another point of light, but this time he felt compelled to look inside, not just because it was near, not just because it was in front of him, because he felt like he needed to, like it was important. Inside this light, Danny saw himself with the team. They celebrated in the locker room, everyone patting him on the back as they passed him.

Through another light he saw the familiar silhouette of Coach, and a strange fear crept through him. He was always a bit apprehensive in Coach's presence, but this was something new, something Danny had only ever felt in the presence of people like the school resource officer.

He swam away, kept looking into light after light

until he finally saw something that didn't make him feel afraid.

Dr. Gunn.

Danny kicked. He remembered he had limbs. He pushed and swam as if moving underwater, and the feel of the space around him began to congeal. It wasn't water, not exactly. It was thicker, moving through it more of a struggle, but he did it. He moved. He pushed himself toward the pinprick of light that held Dr. Gunn and grabbed onto its edges. It felt hot, singed his skin, but Danny refused to let go, refused to let that image of Dr. Gunn spin away into the darkness. He held on tight, looking into the light, into the classroom, at the posters of Malcolm and Martin, of Zora and Langston.

He felt the floor beneath his feet, finally, solid ground, and was grateful for it as his knees quivered, looking into the light. He saw himself in Dr. Gunn's classroom, hand raised, responding silently to one of his questions. The portal of light tried to pull itself away, but Danny held tight to it, feeling his hands singe as he did. He dug his heels into whatever passed for ground, as more light-windows came closer and closer, showing him different images with a frenzy, like they were trying to cover up this one. He shook away images of the football field, of Coach, of the rest of the team in the locker room, of the cheerleaders crowding around him, shook them all away like gnats, finally feeling himself getting angry. The interfering lights pestered him enough to make him finally let go of the one he held, and Dr. Gunn and his classroom spiraled away into the darkness.

Danny had finally had enough, but he felt something different inside him when the anger hit. Something that wasn't shame, something that made him force it down. It was a voice, a distant voice, one that told him it was okay this time. It was okay to lose his temper. It was okay to smash something when what needed destruction was the way the entire world kept you in a cage, in a mold. It's okay to be mad. It's okay to be angry. It's okay to be these things and to be a black kid at the same time.

You have every good goddamn reason to be.

Danny screamed and the darkness around him shattered. Enormous cracks ruptured its surface, both near and far. He felt the darkness shift under his feet and stomped down, sending more fissures cracking through it. There was a huge moan, like the settling of a house at night, like something monstrous stirring awake, and Danny stomped again. He stumbled through the shaking darkness to a nearby crack that ran so far up he couldn't see where or if it ever terminated. He struck out with his sneaker and kicked it, sending tendrils snaking in every direction. He punched it, creating even more. He felt the world buckle underneath his fists, his feet, as huge chunks of glass came falling down around him. Danny looked around as he kicked and fought his way out of this world of darkness, aware that there was something *behind* it all, something large and moving, but the world was shaking too much, he could hardly tell.

Danny hauled back and put everything he had into a single, final, powerful haymaker, a punch that held all his bottled-up rage and frustrations, that destroyed the world around him.

That set him free.

Chapter Seven
The Monster

Kennedy slowly stepped backward. Every face in the room was turned towards her. Every eyeless, mouthless face. She stepped back, but found them behind her as well, the masses penning her in. And then they reached for her. Just as Coach reached for her.

"Sorry, J," she said and kicked him in the balls again.

Jason screamed, Coach screamed, and the room shook. It was rocked by a tremor that felt less like the steady rumble of an earthquake and more like the sudden blast of an explosion. All the dancers looked around, and somehow, even without features, Kennedy could read worry in their expressions. The Coach-thing stepped back, pulling Jason with him.

Another rumble shook the room, maybe the entire House, and Kennedy saw dust shake loose from the ceiling.

Another, and fissures appeared in the walls.

Whatever it was, it was coming closer.

Kennedy shouted and fake-charged at Coach, and he backed away from her advance. Another rumble rocked the room, and this time the ground lifted under Kennedy's feet. She threw her arms out to steady herself as dancers fell around her, streamers and decorations dropping from the walls. Many of the faceless dancers simply gave up,buoying Coach and Jason among their ranks as they ran for exit doors that were suddenly, inexplicably there. Kennedy reached, couldn't let that thing get away with Jason in tow, but the crowd was simply too big.

The pounding came closer, became more and more frequent. Chunks broke away from the ceiling and Kennedy could see through the cracks in the walls to the nothingness beyond. It didn't look like anything. Like infinite darkness. A starless space. There was another blow, and that was when Kennedy realized the nature of the sounds. She thought at first they might've been footsteps, but she was wrong.

They were punches.

Something was pushing its way through the House. Something that terrified its inhabitants.

Another punch. The dancers had almost completely fled the auditorium. Kennedy saw the woman in the distance, pushed along by the throng of bodies desperate to escape. They made eye contact for a moment and something passed between them. A sweetness. A softness. A what-could-have-been.

And as she witnessed Coach dragging Jason away, the entire room crumbled around them.

Danny kept punching and punching. It felt like he was going to bring down the entire world, and he would if he had to. A huge chunk of the sky-painted wall to his right fell away, and Danny saw something long and reptilian whiplash its way out of sight beyond. A huge crack appeared above him, and beyond it he caught a look at something enormous and fleshy, pulsating. He told himself not to look, to focus purely on getting out before everything came down around his ears.

He pushed his way through the wall in front of him, star-speckled sky folding like cardboard, and squeezed himself into a small crevice through which he could see actual light. Danny pushed his way through, listening to the rumble in the room behind him, the shaking groan as everything crumbled. He forced himself through the tiny space, moving sideways towards the light, toward what he somehow knew was true escape.

Before it was blocked.

By Kennedy.

It was her. Really her. There was something in her eyes, how clear they were compared to the visions of Coach and the players and everyone else Danny had seen in this strange place. It was the way she moved, and how she smiled, despite the situation, how it was a smile without the horrid, yellowed teeth everyone else here possessed. It was all those little parts that added up to human.

"Gimme your hand!" Kennedy shouted, leaning against the edge of the small crevice and holding one hand ... down? It took Danny a moment, but he saw the way her ponytail hung, how her necklaces dangled straight towards him, and he felt the sudden and inexplicable shift of gravity in his gut. He wasn't sidling, but suddenly climbing, *slipping*, and he braced himself against the sides of what was not a thin hall anymore but a canyon.

Against every instinct in his brain, Danny's body made him look down, and he instantly regretted it. Below him was an endless black, smoking tendrils reaching up as if to grab him. He looked back up, for a moment horrified that Kennedy might not be there, but she still was, still reaching, and Danny summoned every last bit of strength he had to climb, to reach, to take her proffered hand, and he climbed and Kennedy pulled, and together they hauled him up and out of the canyon as the strange fissure closed behind him.

Kennedy pulled Danny up and out of the fissure, and back into the gymnasium. The place had been trashed. It looked like it did after any dance, magnified by a dozen. All the decorations were destroyed, balloons popped, streamers stripped and lying everywhere. Even the raised stage on which the homecoming thrones sat looked like it had been the victim of some axe murderer, chops and slices running its length.

Jason was on his hands and knees at the edge of the stage, panting and sweating.

"No, no," he said, shaking his head, but his voice wasn't his. It was distorted, doubled, another overlapping his own. "This isn't right. This isn't the way it was supposed to be!"

Behind him, slumped in the throne, was some impossible, horrible thing.

It was a monster. There was simply no other way to describe it. A horrific, skinny creature with pointed, goblin-like ears, jaundice-yellow skin and the bulging potbelly Danny often saw on those infomercials of starving kids in faraway countries. It was so rail-thin Danny thought there was no way it could possibly be alive. It reminded him of animatronic skeletons in Halloween rides, and yet it moved. It gripped the armrests of the throne with a wiry strength Danny could see through its thin skin. Its fingers and toes were tipped with long, dark claws that contrasted sharply against its yellowed skin, through which ran odd, scaly ridges and bumps. Its eyes were dark, but terrifyingly sentient, like it was completely aware of everything happening now, the complexity of this moment, and the events of the night that led them all here. But the worst thing, by far, the worst thing about the creature, was its face. It was humanoid, but its entire nose was something elephantine, stretching out and away from the face into some horrid parody of a trunk, which was much more muscular than the rest of the emaciated body. It looked like a thick anaconda slithering out of the thing's face, covered in the same sharp ridges and barbs that dotted the rest of the body.

That trunk stretched out, away from the thing, and was clamped onto the back of Jason's neck.

Beneath the trunk, the monster smiled at them with that all-too-familiar horrible yellow grin.

Danny and Kennedy could see the trunk pulse and throb, bobbing, the musculature tensing from Jason, who bled under the thing's grasp, moving along the trunk, and back to the monster.

It was sucking on him like a giant leech.

"Get it off," Jason said, in his own voice, from somewhere far away, eyes glazed, not entirely aware of the moment. His veins were blue-black, peeking through his skin. Sweat glazed his body and he swatted aimlessly, drunkenly, behind him. "Guys ... there's something ..."

Danny's hands were around the monster's trunk before he even had time to think about it. The barbs cut into his palm, his fingers, but he didn't care. His anger at Jason vanished. Was he mad at the guy? Sure. Did he want to kick his ass sometimes? Absolutely. But he didn't want him dead. He didn't want him ... whatever this was. This was no way for anybody to be. Danny felt other hands around his own, and for a moment expected the monster, expected it trying to pry him off, but Kennedy stood beside him, grip tight. She nodded at him, ready to go. Danny held the barbed trunk in both hands and planted a foot in the middle of Jason's back. Kennedy followed suit.

"This is gonna hurt, pal."

Together, they pulled.

Jason screamed as the trunk tore away from the back of his neck with a sickening sucking sound, whipping around and spraying blood-yellow viscera like an unattended garden hose on full blast. Danny and Kennedy let it go and reached for Jason, covering themselves against the spray as they pulled him down and off the stage. Behind them, the creature shrieked and roared, its trunk flailing, spewing pus and goo everywhere. The world rumbled around them like they were in a dollhouse shaken by an angry toddler.

"Run!" Danny shouted to Kennedy as he knelt down and hauled Jason up and over his shoulder, carrying him like a fireman might carry a wounded person. Kennedy ran ahead as the walls around them shifted and bent at the unnatural angles of a Tim Burton movie. Decorations were thrown to the floor and huge chunks of tile broke away, chasing after the kids in their fall like giant sets of teeth clamping shut behind them. Kennedy shoved the double doors ahead of them open just as an enormous fissure erupted across the gymnasium wall. Danny looked for only a moment and regretted it; behind the wall, there was something enormous and fleshy, a wall of skin and meat behind the illusion of the gym, something large and writhing, that spasmed as the House shook.

"Come on!" Kennedy screamed, holding the door open and waving him ahead. Beyond her was a short hallway, but one that belonged in a house, not a school, and Danny hauled ass toward her, running fast but running careful. He crossed the threshold with Jason and Kennedy ran ahead, pushing the next door, the front door, open.

And they all ran out into the light.

The fluorescent lights of the Northfield Mall were warm in comparison to the interior of the House. Danny never thought he'd miss those strange, cold, impersonal lights. But as he and Kennedy, with Jason in tow, burst out of Gorman's House and into the Northfield Mall food court, he rejoiced. They hit the tile floor, but kept running. It wasn't just the sounds coming from behind them, the obvious crumbling, but the entire ordeal. Everything made them want to put as much distance between themselves and Gorman's House as possible. Not until they were halfway down one of the wings of the mall, past the Spencer's Gifts, did they slow. And even then, only out of exhaustion, out of simply not being able to run anymore. Danny dropped to his knees, letting Jason down as gently as he could, checking that he was still breathing before he turned and followed Kennedy's look over his shoulder.

Gorman's House was collapsing. The building was falling in on itself. Cleanly, neatly, like a professional demolition. Its three floors fell inward, a giant, sucking breath pulling it all down as glass shattered and timbers snapped like bones until it was nothing more than an unidentifiable pile of detritus.

They found an emergency telephone down one of the maintenance hallways. Kennedy called the police while Danny stayed with Jason. He managed to get him lucid and to stop the bleeding from the wound on the back of his neck.

"You alright?" Danny asked.

Jason looked at him, but said nothing, simply holding the compress, a shirt stolen from the nearby Old Navy, against the back of his neck.

Kennedy came back and said the police and ambulances were on their way.

"There could be more people inside," she said, looking past Danny and Jason to the ruins of Gorman's House. She said it, but she didn't sound very hopeful.

"What did you tell them?" Danny asked, wondering how in the world they could ever explain something like this.

"I just said there was an accident," Kennedy said.

At the ruins of the House, the front door still stood.

Chapter Eight
Adulthood

I t wasn't long before Northfield Mall was bustling with activity again. There was so much light and noise it must've vaguely approximated the mall on a Saturday night in the glory days of the 1980s. Police cars and ambulances had somehow gotten themselves into the mall itself, parked in front of the FYE and the Victoria's Secret and the Panda Express where, not too long ago, shoppers strolled.

The medics pulled Jason into the back of the ambulance and were examining his wound. Firefighters had begun a search of the ruins of Gorman's House. The police were talking to Kennedy, and tried to talk to Danny, who did exactly what his father, what his mother, Dr. Gunn, what every black adult in his life told him to do; he didn't talk to the police until his parents got there. And when Kennedy saw his silence in the face of their questions, she did the same, standing next to him, saying nothing except that she didn't want to say anything until her parents were there.

A few minutes before their parents arrived on the scene, a detective in a slick jacket waved the uniformed police officers away. He plopped down in one of the food court chairs with the same kind of nonchalance he would as if he'd just picked up his Panda Express lunch. He waited with them, let them talk to their parents after they arrived, let them talk to themselves, was apparently in no rush at all. Like he saw this kind of thing every day.

"What are we supposed to say happened?" Danny asked in a rare moment where the three of them were left alone, their parents talking amongst themselves, the detective doodling something in his notepad.

"The truth," Jason said.

Danny and Kennedy looked at him like he'd just suggested they confess to taking handfuls of mushrooms and going on joyrides in a stolen cop car. Jason held up his hands in surrender.

"We don't know," Kennedy said, spinning a plan on the fly. Hoping it worked. "I mean … do we?"

"We found an invitation," Danny said. "We showed up here."

"People in masks chased us," Kennedy continued.

"It's Halloween," Jason said, getting with the program. "There could have been all kinds of trickery."

Danny said, "We don't know how they did it."

"They'll want the cartridge," Kennedy said.

Danny scoffed. "They can have it. I never wanna see that thing again."

And so they told their story, and so the detective wrote it down, and the legend of Gorman's House had one more chapter added to it.

Epilogue

Somewhere, in an undisclosed location, a place redacted on dozens of different government documents, a place that didn't officially exist, but whose location was known only to upper management, there stood a door. Stood, because that is exactly what the door did. It was not placed in a wall, did not cover up a threshold. It simply stood there in the middle of a large, empty, but certainly not unsupervised, room. Scattered all around the room were CCTV cameras, cameras recording to multiple VHS tapes and redundant drives backed up in multiple locations. Watermarked across the bottom of those recorded images were the words PROPERTY OF THE BUREAU OF SPECIAL SER-

VICES. CLASSIFIED.

Those same images were stamped onto a wooden box that contained an unmarked video game cartridge. A cartridge that was put into storage in a vast, underground room with dozens, hundreds of other boxes, and locked up in a secure vault deep below the earth.

Monday morning, Danny walked into Dr. Gunn's classroom long before the bell for first period rang. He took a seat at the front of the class.

"Mr. Green," Dr. Gunn said, surprised, looking up from grading papers. He stood up and circled his desk, leaned against it like he always did during lectures. "I heard about what happened on Halloween. Are you and your friends alright?"

Danny had wandered around Beacon long enough to hear the rumors, to hear the story, the legend, that was solidifying around the events of Halloween weekend. Someone, or some group of someones, was supposed to have staged a pop-up event based on the Gorman's House legend. But they'd used it all as an excuse for some nefarious spree killing. All allegedly, of course. They didn't find any bodies beneath Gorman's House, but there were at least a dozen people from Beacon who'd gone missing on Halloween night. Someone said the police had crime scene sketches of the alleged perpetrators, though Danny couldn't imagine where they might have gotten them from, or how wrong they possibly were.

"We're getting there," Danny said, which was true. They were all on their way to okay, but at different places.

"I can't imagine you'll be playing in the homecoming game," Dr. Green said.

"No, no, I won't," Danny told him. "But that's because I quit the team."

A long moment of silence passed between them, one where Danny could tell Dr. Green was trying to suss out whether this was good news or bad.

Danny took out a pencil. "I'm here to retake your test, sir."

Dr. Green smiled.

"Of course, son."

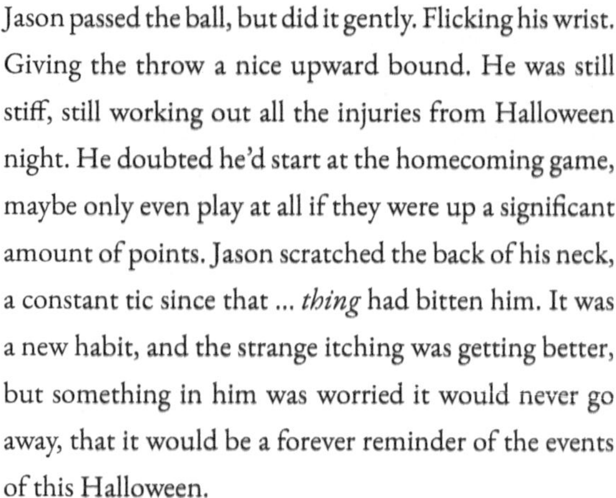

Jason passed the ball, but did it gently. Flicking his wrist. Giving the throw a nice upward bound. He was still stiff, still working out all the injuries from Halloween night. He doubted he'd start at the homecoming game, maybe only even play at all if they were up a significant amount of points. Jason scratched the back of his neck, a constant tic since that ... *thing* had bitten him. It was a new habit, and the strange itching was getting better, but something in him was worried it would never go away, that it would be a forever reminder of the events of this Halloween.

Jason caught the returned ball and looked to the sidelines, saw Danny pass by on his way to the parking lot. They gave one another the classic high school jock nod, because what else could they do? What else could capture everything that had happened between them? They'd talked about it a few times, with Kennedy, and after handing over the cartridge that got them all into that mess, they hadn't heard from the police. Things had gone silent. It was over.

Jason saw Coach giving Danny a mean mug as he

passed by, and before he could stop himself, before he even thought about the repercussions, he lobbed the football and popped Coach in the shoulder. Hard enough to send a message, but soft enough to say this was—probably—an accident.

"Sorry, Coach!" Jason shouted, his teammates trying to hide giggles all around him. He spun his arm around in the socket as Coach sucked in a huge breath, looked like he was about to yell something before he must've remembered the story of Halloween night.

"Just watch that arm," he growled, before moving downfield.

Jason looked over at Danny, who smiled.

"Just hold onto me, okay? We're gonna take things nice and easy."

Kennedy knew that Ryan was aware of how clammy her hands were. She knew Ryan could see the fear and excitement in her eyes. She held onto Kennedy's forearms, keeping her balanced, as Kennedy took two tentative steps up onto the skateboard.

"There," Ryan said, looking down at Kennedy's feet and then up into her eyes. "Easy, isn't it?"

"Yeah," Kennedy breathed, looking down at her feet so she wouldn't be tempted to look at Ryan. The temptation proved to be too much. "Easy."

"Okay, just hold still," Ryan said, circling her, keeping her hands on her, and coming around behind her. She held Kennedy's hips. "Now we're just gonna move forward slowly, okay?"

"Okay," Kennedy said, resisting the urge to reach down and hold Ryan's hands. It was easy when her body demanded balance. She kept her arms wide out at her sides like she was going to try to fly. "Aaaaand, we're off!"

Ryan pushed her forward, and Kennedy might as well have been flying.

Acknowledgements

There are genuinely too many people to thank for helping to bring any book to life, so if you've helped with this book and your name doesn't appear here, please check the back of my neck and make sure the proboscis of some bizarre vampire isn't attached to me.

Firstly, a huge thanks to Joey and Mad Axe Media for taking a chance on a then-unproven writer and for taking the first book I ever sold on pitch!

A huge thanks to everyone who helped get the word out about this book, the early readers, blurbers, and ARC reviewers, JV Gachs, Chloe Spencer, Wendy Dalrymple, Rachel Bolton, Ally Russell, Kristen Rogers-Anderson, Rebecca White, Adam Allen, and I'm sure there will be plenty more who help me out after this acknowledgment page is written.

Thank you to my homies in the HWG and the GT-TUnit for always keeping things spooky and fun, to my brothers, for going on childhood adventures into the woods and through drainage pipes and down rivers and abandoned lots and all the other insane stuff we got up to. We have shenaned before and we will shenan again.

Thank you to my wife, for watching a bunch of analog horror with me to help me get in the mood.

And, finally, a huge thanks to my dad for giving me a childhood that made this book possible. Thanks for letting me check out all those horror VHSs from Blockbuster when Mom wasn't looking. Mom, I swear they didn't traumatize me, despite what you may have just read.

About the author

TT Madden (they/them) is a Pushcart-nominated, genderfluid, mixed-race writer who refuses to keep "politics" out of their writing. They've written in the sandboxes of big IPs, helping create the *Blair Witch* tabletop mystery game for Hunt a Killer, but they much prefer writing smaller, weirder stories that make you uncomfortable, but in a way you hopefully want to explore more. Their short prose has been published by Ghoulish Tales, Bag of Bones Press, and Speculation Publications, among others. Their novellas have been published by Off Limits Press, Neon Hemlock, and Little Ghost Books, with more forthcoming. They can be found at ttmaddenwrites.carrd.co when they're not wandering the woods around their home, looking for spooky inspiration.